VENETIAN'S
DARING SEDUCTION

(AN ITALIAN BILLIONAIRES NOVEL)

Jennifer Blake

STEEL MAGNOLIA PRESS

THE VENETIAN'S DARING SEDUCTION

Copyright © 2013, 2016 Patricia Maxwell

Cover Art by Amanda Kelsey of Razzle Dazzle Design

All rights reserved. No part of this publication may be reproduced, stored in a retrieval system, or transmitted by any means—electronic, mechanical, photographic (photocopying), recording, or otherwise—without prior permission in writing from the author, with the exception of brief quotations embodied in critical articles and reviews.

For more information contact:
patriciaamaxwell@bellsouth.net

ISBN: 9781519079251

Chapter One

"Hello there, you handsome devil."

Celina Steadman murmured that greeting to the Venetian gentlemen before her as she leaned in mere inches from his face. He really was a bold figure, the very image of most women's romantic fantasies.

His features were classic, with a wide brow, straight nose, square, almost pugnacious jaw, and high, aristocratic cheekbones. His brows were slashes of black and his lashes thick and curling at the tips, a perfect screen for his thoughts. One corner of his sensuously molded lips seemed about to lift in some secret amusement. A wicked gleam lay in the blackness of his eyes. Their darkness was relieved, however, by golden rays in the irises that echoed the intricate gold braid on his velvet coat.

The wide shoulders of this gorgeous hunk of manhood were cloaked in black silk. A mask dangled from his fingers, one made of gold-painted papier-mâché with a beak-like nose in the style made famous by the great Casanova. Behind him lay the Grand Canal in all its past non-motorized glory, reflecting an aqua blue sky, the softly colored façades and red-tiled roofs of the palazzo which lined it. Conte Lucca di Palladino was perfection against that exotic backdrop. He stared out from it with confidence that bordered on arrogance, supremely certain of his place in that rarified world.

Celina heaved a heartfelt sigh. They didn't make men like him anymore, at least not in her experience. Such a pity.

Bracing against the top of the tall stepladder she was using, she touched the cool, painted canvas of the life-size portrait. She ran a gently questing fingertip along the conte's firm jaw line, caressed the sensual line of his lower lip.

"What a favorite you must have been with the ladies," she told the long-dead Venetian nobleman in wry appreciation. "I'll bet you gave old Casanova a run for his money."

"That is a bet you would lose."

The correction, deep-voiced, faintly accented and none too friendly, came from directly below her.

Celina startled so violently that the ancient ladder wobbled beneath her. She stretched a hand toward the portrait for balance but snatched it back for fear of damaging it. Grabbing at the top step in front of her instead, she clung to it while her heart lurched back and forth in her chest.

"Careful!"

The man below reached up to catch her ankle in a firm grip. A spark like the impact from a Taser surged up her leg. It flared in her lower body and swept onward to jar her brain with the force of a lightning strike. She was still an instant before twisting carefully at the waist to look down.

It was as if the Venetian gentleman in the portrait had come to life. He stared up with a frown of concern on his too-handsome face and one strong hand steadying her stepladder while the other curled firmly around her ankle. Tall, wide of shoulder and with dark brown eyes lit by golden gleams, he was exactly the same.

This man was not in period dress, however, but wore a suit of such perfect fit it had undoubtedly been tailored to his measurements. Paired with it was a shirt so white it seemed to glow against his olive skin. His tie was a symphony of blues and greens, and his shoes were of softly gleaming leather of a quality found only in Italy.

His dark gaze met hers for a moment. Then it drifted leisurely over her, brushing her breasts, waist and hips to linger on the tanned length of her legs that were exposed by the short denim skirt she wore.

"The fact is," he went on as if nothing had happened, "the first Conte di Palladino was a devoted husband who married when he was twenty, gave his contessa nine children in fifteen years, and so mourned her death that he never married again, never looked at another woman."

Celina barely heard him. If he chose to adjust his position beneath her, he might see more of her than she cared to expose. She jolted into movement, descending from her perch with more speed than grace.

"Per l'amor di Dio!" He released her ankle, reaching to put a hand on her hip to halt her progress. "Do you want to break your neck?"

"I'll be fine, thank you, if you'll just step away." She could feel his every fingertip through her clothing, five separate spots of branding heat. She was also far more aware than she wanted to be that she had come to a stop with her backside at the level of his face.

"You are quite certain?" He released her, but only moved to grip both sides of the ladder so she was enclosed by the cage of his arms. She could feel the heat of his body surrounding her, caught the delicious hints of expensive aftershave in combination with clean linen and warm male. An odd dizziness swept over, one that had little to do with her uncertain perch.

"Yes, of course. I was—you just startled me." She twisted at the waist to look down at him again. He was close, so close.

"I don't doubt it, as you seemed about to make off with one of my ancestors."

"Yours?"

He inclined his head. "I am Lucca Palladino."

Of course he was, and named for his ancestor, apparently. She might have known. "You're Signor Palladino's grandson, then."

He frowned, perhaps at this proof that she had some acquaintance with his grandfather who owned the painting and the palazzo where it hung. "And who would you be? Other than a woman who holds conversations with men long dead?"

"The person hired by your grandfather to appraise his art collection. And I was neither holding a conversation with the conte nor stealing him. I was only—"

"Showing your approval, I believe. I'm sure he would have appreciated it."

Oh, there—*there*—was the wicked glint of amusement the artist had caught so well. It was stunning in the flesh, a blatant invitation to share in the absurdity of life. It was also an unfair distraction when she was trying to hold on to her annoyance.

"Such a paragon of fidelity? Surely not."

"He was faithful, not dead." He tipped his head in consideration. "Well, not at the time anyway. But how am I to accept what you say? You appear too young to be responsible for such a valuable appraisal."

"That is something between me and your grandfather." She backed down another step as she spoke, thinking he would move aside to give her room.

It was a mistake. He didn't shift an inch, and her change of position put her breasts uncomfortably close to his mouth as she half-turned again to look at him. Hot color seeped upward from under the neckline of her blue sweater, rising to her hairline.

"Indeed?" he asked in soft inquiry as his gaze narrowed on her features. "And how is it that you know him?"

"I don't. He contacted the auction house where I work

and requested my services."

"Did he now? How *very* enterprising of him."

"Not that kind of services!" she snapped, as irritated with herself for leaving an opening for such a suggestive remark as for the subtle innuendo in his voice. The ease with which he used it was an indication of the excellence of his English, however. That he spoke to her in that language was doubtless because he'd heard her talking to his ancestor.

"How is it he heard of you?"

"An article in the magazine put out by the auction house, I believe."

"An American auction house."

"Exactly. Is that a problem?"

"He saw it, he called and you came. Just like that."

She stared at him in exasperation. "It is how these things work, after all."

"You're certain."

"I was offered the job, and I accepted it. If you need to know more, ask your grandfather."

It wasn't really that simple, but Lucca Palladino didn't need to know the details. While it was true the auction house where she worked had dispatched her to Venice after a direct request, she had read up on the present Conte Massimo Palladino well before then and suggested a solicitation for an appraisal be emailed to him. It was possible there was a connection of sorts between them, but it was too fantastic to mention. Certainly, she had not breathed a word of it to Signor Palladino on her arrival the day before.

She might never mention it. It all depended on what she discovered now she was in Venice.

"Italy is overrun with art experts," the conte's grandson said. "What need had my nonno, my grandfather, to look abroad for one, particularly when you can have little practical experience?"

"And I'm a female, too. Don't forget that," she added with a lift of her chin.

"No. How could I?"

The rich timbre of his voice with its hint of an accent did strange things to her heartbeat. His breath fanned across the scooped neck of her sweater, causing a rash of goose bumps that disappeared under the fabric, sweeping over her breasts so her nipples contracted into small knots. She was glad beyond words that her bra concealed that reaction. Though she wondered if it was entirely successful, given the brief glance Lucca Palladino gave her top where its teal lace peeped above the scooped neck.

She refused to check, however, just as she refused to be held a prisoner. With jerky determination, she descended the last two steps to the floor.

He still did not release the ladder, nor did he back away. She was far too close as she turned to face him, her breasts practically pressed against his chest, her gaze upon the strong, brown column of his neck before she lifted it to his mouth. Its firm edges and smooth surfaces made it an exact replica of his ancestor's in the portrait. All trace of humor was gone, however. The lips of the present conte's grandson were set in a hard, determined line.

"I think," he said in a low growl that sent his warm breath filtering through her hair, "that it will be best if I take a look at your credentials."

She swallowed hard, even as her heart doubled its beat. She held a degree in art history and had been working at the auction house for three years, but could boast no special expertise. "My credentials?"

"As an appraiser of art, of course. What else?"

She didn't know what else; that was the problem. Something about his intent expression as he watched her suggested a different meaning. Or her imagination might be working overtime, influenced by his uncanny likeness to a portrait that had enthralled her moments before. Could she really be so thrown off balance by a handsome face and autocratic manner?

"The arrangement for my work here is with your grandfather," she said with an edge to her voice. "I don't see that it has anything to do with you."

"What concerns him, concerns me." He eased closer so his thighs brushed hers into tingling awareness of his hard strength and her own soft vulnerability. "I will not allow anyone to take advantage of him, least of all a woman young enough to be his granddaughter."

"As if I would!" A shiver trickled down her spine at that description of her.

"No, for I will prevent it. No matter what it takes."

~ ~ ~

The words had barely left Lucca's mouth before the woman

he was holding bent her head and swiftly ducked from under his arms where he'd imprisoned her against the stepladder. Whirling, she backed away from him. Triumph flashed across her face, lighting eyes that shone with the same greenish blue of the Adriatic that fed the canals of Venice.

He almost laughed at how pleased she was to escape him. No doubt she thought him defeated. It would be a pleasure to show her otherwise.

His grandfather, Lucca knew, was old-fashioned, tender of heart and easily taken in by feminine guile. He had a special weakness for blondes, as well, particularly the shining, natural blonde of this appraiser of art whose hair seemed to be made from sunlight. Lucca was not impressed. No, not even if his fingers did itch to discover if the shimmering tresses that swung so freely around her head and shoulders were as silky soft as they appeared. Or if he'd actually caught the gleam of iridescent beads braided into its thickness.

He was also painfully aware of the symmetrical curves under the plain skirt and sweater she wore, of the splendor of her long, shapely legs and also the turn of her ankle that had fit so easily in his grasp.

It had been a wrench to release her. As he stood so near her moments ago, it had taken considerable control to keep from moving closer until she was pressed fully against him. That need plagued him still, dragging at his temper.

He glanced at the diver's watch on his wrist. His grandfather would be resting just now, along with most of Venice at this hour. No doubt that was why this so-called appraiser from the States felt free to wander about the palazzo, checking out centuries of artwork collected by his family, not to mention the ancestor portraits that lined the walls here in the main salon.

She had not been on the premises when he left for his meeting in Milan two days ago, so could not be seriously entrenched. He didn't know how she'd gotten her hooks into his grandfather, but he wasn't about to let her sink them deeper. If he moved quickly, he should be able to get rid of her before any damage was done. Giovanni was putting the powerboat away after picking him up at the Piazzale Roman on his return, but it could be brought around again.

"Where are you staying?" he asked in abrupt decision. "I expect you would like to return to your hotel for your afternoon rest. Someone can take you now."

"I don't believe…." She trailed off as she glanced past his shoulder. Her eyes brightened while relief flooded her face.

"No, indeed," his grandfather said from behind him. "Where are your manners, Lucca? The young lady is staying here, of course."

Alarm coursed along Lucca's veins. His grandfather enjoyed having people around him, but his most bountiful hospitality was reserved for family. Conte Massimo Palladino did not invite strangers into his home, particularly strange young women. He also rested well past this hour every afternoon. There was more here than met the eye.

"Naturally, Nonno, if you say so," he said, turning to face Massimo, inclining his head in a gesture of respect.

His chest tightened at once. His grandfather was dressed with special care, in fine cashmere trousers in soft gray, a pale cream shirt, with a loosely tied scarf in gray and cream at his throat. His silver hair was brushed within an inch of its life, and he stood straight and tall, with his shoulders back and his stomach sucked in as flat as it was possible to make it.

The changes were obviously for the benefit of his guest. The conte did not go to such trouble for a mere grandson. It was another red flag.

"You have met Signorina Celina Steadman?" Massimo smiled upon the young woman with pleasure in his lined face. "My grandson introduced himself to you?"

"We met, yes," she answered. Lucca half expected her to complain about the way she had been greeted, but she said no more.

"Excellent, excellent." Massimo rubbed his hands together with a dry, papery sound. "I thought you would not see each other until dinner, but this is better. Shall we have coffee in the loggia?"

"By all means," Lucca said at once, "unless the signorina will be too cool?"

It was a test if Celina Steadman but knew it. A watery sun had been coming and going behind gray clouds all day. Regardless, the loggia fronting on the Grand Canal would catch the full effect of the notoriously chill wind off the water, with its damp hint of coming rain. Would she sacrifice comfort to please the man who had employed her?

An impish light sprang into her greenish-blue eyes as she answered. "I'm sure I'll survive. Winters in New England aren't what you might call balmy."

She not only recognized his challenge but was inclined to accept it. There was a brain beneath the blonde hair, one that might well be as devious as it was quick. He must not be misled by her sense of fair play or her smiles.

The loggia opened off the salon where they stood. It was floored with ochre stone and fronted by a solid balustrade of the same material. At each end were stone pots overflowing with the wiry and leafless canes of roses that would bloom there come summer. The walls at one end of the palazzo were concealed by steel scaffolding enclosed with heavy gray plastic, however—a signature of the constant restoration in Venice.

Sergio, his grandfather's quietly efficient manservant of many years, brought small cups of espresso and biscotti flavored with almond and cardamom, serving them on the teakwood table with its cloth of golden yellow embroidered in red. Without being asked, he added cream for the lady, as if he'd already learned her preferences, and also an aperitif of berry-flavored liqueur against the coolness of the day. He retreated then, closing the French doors of the salon behind him, though whether from discretion or for the sake of warmth it was impossible to say.

"Well now," Massimo said expansively as he leaned back in his chair with his cup in his hand, "isn't this pleasurable."

"Definitely." Celina smiled as her gaze drifted over the

line of palazzi that faced them across the canal. "I can't believe I'm actually here."

"It's your first time in Venice then." Lucca watched her with care as he sipped the rich brew in his cup.

"Yes, though I've dreamed of it for years."

"So my grandfather made your dream come true." He glanced at Massimo who was watching Celina with something like fascination in his eyes.

"As it happens. And of course, I could not be more grateful."

"It is our very great honor to have you here, *cara*," Massimo said. He glanced at Lucca. "Celina is quite an authority in her field, you know. She was written up in a most prestigious magazine after finding a Canaletto in someone's attic. Her comments in the article showed an amazing knowledge of the artist's work."

"Indeed." Lucca's alarm tightened another notch as he noted the mild endearment his grandfather had used with practiced ease.

"You're too kind," she said with a quick smile, a hint of color rising to her cheekbones.

Massimo shook his head. "It was quite masterful, full of detail on the least-known years of his career and his lesser canvases. I learned things I'd never heard before."

"I was more than a little enthused, wasn't I?" she said with a wry chuckle. "Though the most interesting thing about the painting I found, beyond the signature and artistry, was the dedication on the back."

"Dedication?" Lucca lifted a brow.

"Very simple, but telling, or so I thought. It said only, 'Forever.'"

"That's where you heard about the signorina, in this journal?" Lucca asked as his grandfather's slow shake of his white, leonine head drew his attention. Canaletto's work was a passion for him. Several examples of it hung throughout the palazzo. It was difficult to believe anything Celina Steadman had learned about this quintessential Venetian painter could be unknown in Venice.

"Actually, I read the article on the Internet," Nonno answered.

"You hired Signorina Steadman on the strength of it then."

"She also came highly recommended by the auction house that employs her."

The comment carried a fondness that sounded ominous. Moreover, his grandfather was still watching his guest instead of giving his attention to the questions. It was all Lucca could do to keep his voice even as he spoke again. "And that was all?"

"I believe your grandson is inquiring about my credentials again." Celina reached for a slice of biscotti that had been drizzled with chocolate. The movement stretched her sweater across her breasts, outlining their tender shape in a way that made Lucca's mouth water against his will.

"Surely not," Massimo answered at his most gallant. "He must know a lovely lady needs none."

Lucca was saved from a reply by the roar of a passing bus-like *vaporetto* crowded with passengers. The waves of its rolling wake slapped the wall of the *fondamenta,* the walkway directly below them, before cascading down in a wash of foam. A water taxi sped past in the opposite direction, while following along behind that was an open boat so laden with bathroom fixtures it rode dangerously low in the water.

He caught himself watching the look of pleasure on Celina Steadman's face as her gaze followed the common *vaporetto.* It was all new to her, of course, but hardly as fascinating as she seemed to find it. There was no need for her to turn a smile of such unalloyed pleasure upon his grandfather. No need at all.

They were in such charity with each other it set Lucca's teeth on edge.

His grandfather was not a fool, nor was he senile. It was not like him to fall prey to feminine wiles. How had this Celina Steadman gotten so close so quickly?

She seemed a typical American, attractive in a natural, forthright manner; she was certainly no femme fatale.

Yet she carried an impact, Lucca had to admit. Even he felt it, like a shaft of sunlight in winter, one so warm it caused a slow burn in his groin. The soft surfaces of her lips drew his gaze against his will, while the melodic rise and fall of her voice in her native English made him want to move closer as he listened. Was it possible he was overreacting merely because she disturbed him?

But no, the conte was clearly besotted. The feeling seemed oddly mutual, too. Celina's expression when she looked at his nonno held a hint of warm affection that should not have been there. It was inappropriate for a business association with a man she'd just met, much less one three times her age.

Had they known each other longer than it appeared? Could this be one of those Internet affairs that had blossomed into an invitation to visit?

Why hide behind the pretense of art appraising then? It wasn't as if his grandfather couldn't have a virtual fling if he wanted it.

No, there was something else going on here. Lucca didn't know what it was, but he intended to find out before he was many days older.

Chapter Two

*P*erfect, everything was so perfect, Celina thought. She loved all of it—the gray sky reflecting in the choppy water of the canal so it had the look of hammered pewter, the surging water traffic that splashed waves against the blue-and-white striped poles marking water entrances, the wonderful old buildings with their red-tiled roofs above façades of marble and travertine, or else stucco in peach and rust, cream and gold.

The photographs she'd seen, and even Canaletto's paintings, hadn't done it justice. They couldn't include the myriad shades of blue in the shadows upon the water cast by buildings, the dampness of the breeze or the dank yet intriguing scent of the canal that was in constant motion beneath where they sat.

The water level was closer than she had expected, so close the spray from the waves dampened the bottom of the balustrade. It made the canal seem more intimate somehow, as if it was a part of life in the palazzo. The grand old building itself was like a fairytale castle with its high ceilings, long galleries, stone columns that swirled like swizzle sticks and floors of different-colored marbles set in geometrical patterns. She had not yet explored all the artwork, but what she had seen hinted at untold delights.

She'd feared she would be disappointed in Conte Massimo Palladino. Instead, she was completely charmed. He was just as she had expected an Italian gentleman of his years to be: kind, courteous, and altogether engaging.

The only problem was his grandson.

The count had mentioned Lucca in their few phone conversations; he was obviously proud of him and his accomplishments. He was also happy to have him under his roof still, even if he had said the two of them rattled around in the huge place like a couple of windup soldiers left behind in a toy box. She'd known Lucca lived on the premises then. Being so near her in age, she'd thought he might make her stay easier. She hadn't expected the exact opposite.

"The two of you have much in common," Massimo said as he glanced between her and his grandson. "Lucca is an architect specializing in preservation of the valuable old palazzi of Venice, Celina, as I might have mentioned before. He works closely with the *Consorzio Venizia Nuova*, the group that safeguards the city, preventing it from sinking into the sea. And, Lucca, our guest not only appraises paintings but restores them, as well as other old things. She is currently renovating a country cottage that belonged to her grandmother."

As a gambit to fill the lapse in conversation, it wasn't bad, Celina thought. On the other hand, it wasn't particularly successful, either.

"*Davvero?*" Lucca said politely as he watched her. "This is so? You must be very busy. It is remarkable you found time in your schedule for travel."

"I make time for things that are important to me," she answered, meeting his dark gaze.

The light in the sky was dimmed by passing clouds, so his face took on a forbidding cast. "And you count my grandfather's art collection among those things."

If there was one thing she couldn't stand, it was judgmental men who assumed the worst where women were concerned. She'd had enough of that growing up, watched enough of it while staying with her grandmother when she was small.

"Of course," she answered in brittle irony. "How could I resist such treasure? The offer of a stay in a real Venetian palazzo was just icing on the cake."

"Of course," he repeated in dry agreement.

"You brighten these old walls, signorina, such as they are," Massimo said with a courteous tilt of his head. As a distraction, perhaps, from the byplay between her and his grandson, he waved at the plastic sheeting that flapped in the wind as it hung from the scaffolding of the palazzo. "You see Lucca's handiwork there, yes?"

Her interest quickened as she glanced at it. "Is there a

serious problem?"

"*Dio*, there must be as we have had this covering of great ugliness in place for months," he said with a grimace. "But you will have to ask Lucca."

"Moss and mold from water seepage, stone carvings decayed by pollution," his grandson said with the lift of one shoulder. "But most serious is the undermining of the soil beneath the walls."

"Actually? Here?" She glanced up and down the loggia where they sat. She'd known of frame houses on the east coast so undercut by storms they caved into the ocean, but the stone around her seemed solid and timeless, as if it should be immune to such ravages.

"You know, I suppose, that Venice was built on an island that has been sinking into the sea ever since? But yes, most people do. A part of it is simple soil erosion and building subsidence, but motor traffic constantly churning the water doesn't help."

"Or water levels rising due to climate change?"

"So some would have it," he conceded. "Sea levels around the world are mounting at a faster rate than in centuries past. The process was once slow, a mere inch or so every hundred years, but that's no longer true."

"The palazzo is really at risk then."

"As is Venice herself. Everything you see around you could be under water one day."

She followed his gesture as it swept toward the houses that lined the canal in front of them. "Reading about it is one thing, but being here turns it into a tragedy. It's all so beautiful, so unique in the world."

"Such is life," Massimo said with a genial smile. "But the process is slow. With luck, I won't be here when it happens."

"Don't say that, Nonno." Lucca's voice was firm.

"Why not, if it's true?"

Celina smiled a little at her host's placid acceptance, but her gaze was still on Lucca. "It must be satisfying work, to put off the inevitable as long as possible."

Surprise flashed in his eyes before he turned his attention to the coffee cup in hand. "It has its moments."

The older man's gaze turned intent as he watched them. "You must take Celina on a tour of the city, Lucca," he said in mild suggestion. "She should see something of Venice while here, and you could point out more of the projects you have in hand."

"Oh, but I should get back to work," she objected.

"I would be delighted." Lucca spoke at the same time, his voice even.

Celina gave him a quick glance. There was nothing in his face except polite agreement, but she was sure playing escort to her tourist was the last thing he wanted.

She wasn't at all sure she wanted it either. Though she was eager to explore and would be glad of a guide, she couldn't think time spent with Massimo's stand-offish grandson would be much fun. No matter how to-die-for good-looking he might be.

"*Bene,*" Massimo said. "Rain is predicted over the next few days, and who knows when it may start. It is better that you go now."

The powerboat was long, sleek and detailed with red stripes on white, the Venetian version of a limousine with its glassed-in cabin fitted with bucket seats in red leather. The driver, Giovanni, brought it around to the palazzo's landing with great panache, gunning the engine, minutely adjusting the steering to hold it in place. His grin was cheerful and approving as he watched Lucca hand Celina inside. She was barely seated and Lucca on board before he swerved away from the water step and skimmed into the traffic that crowded the Grand Canal.

It was a noisy yet exhilarating ride as they dodged water taxis and big ungainly *vaporetti,* tourist gondolas and boats piled high with TVs, stacks of wood framing and sacks of potatoes. Ornate marble bridges flew past overhead, and they skimmed around wide curves, bouncing over the wakes of other crafts. Celina leaned against the window, staring up at the fantastically carved and decorated façades of houses and churches, unable to stop smiling as she saw vendors set up along the *fondamenta* selling newspapers and magazines, umbrellas and scarves and fantastically ornate masks for the *carnevale* season that was nearly upon them. She watched the gulls that cried as they wheeled overhead and the flocks of pigeons that spiraled up out of hidden squares, or campos.

"You haven't traveled much?" Lucca asked, breaking the silence that held them.

She flashed a grin in his direction. "Only in the States. Is it so obvious?"

"You seem to be enjoying it."

"As I said before, I've been waiting all my life to come here."

"*Certo?* For sure? All your life?"

"Most of it, anyway. My grandmother used to tell such stories about it. I used to beg to hear them, over and over again." She shouldn't tell him that, she was sure, but it was so strong in her memory just now.

"She visited often then."

"Only a few weeks out of one summer, but she saw so much, did so much, in that short time."

"A flower child, I suppose, one of the many who backpacked through Europe in those days."

The hint of disparagement in his voice touched her on the raw. "An art student, actually."

"I see."

"I doubt that. She gained a certain amount of fame as an artist in her later years, after my grandfather died. She was particularly well-known for her ability to capture pure light and water reflections."

"Then she made good use of her time here."

Her darling Grandma Marilee had done that, Celina knew, though she had not realized the extent of it until she inherited her country cottage after she died. There had been journals, stacks of them, hidden away in the attic, some detailing her girlhood, some the barren nature of her marriage. One of them described the days of her Italian sojourn, where she'd gone, what she'd seen and enjoyed, and with whom.

"I suppose she did."

"As you are doing."

Anger stirred inside her and she met his dark gaze. "What do you mean by that?"

"You seem to have made yourself at home at the palazzo."

She stared at him while hot color burned in her cheeks. What he'd said was certainly plain speaking. Fine, she could do that. "It's clear you don't like that I'm here. What I don't get is why. What is it to you?"

"It's nothing to me. You are my grandfather's guest, not mine."

His mouth was set in grim lines. It was an expression she'd seen often in her early life, an indication of a mind just as tightly closed. That she could notice such a thing at a time like this, especially the intriguing way his upper lip closed on the sensual fullness of the lower, did nothing to soothe her temper.

"Oh, well, then you won't care if I move in on dear old gramps while I'm here," she said, injecting breezy challenge into her voice. "You'll be more than okay with it if I wind up as your grandmother?"

His face darkened and his espresso-black eyes snapped with ill humor. "Don't be ridiculous."

"It does sound foolish when you put it that way, doesn't it? Though it seems to be what you believe I'm doing."

"I never said so."

"You didn't, did you?" A corner of her mouth curled in a wry smile. "But I don't know what else to think, can't see why you're so negative. Your grandfather verified how I came to be here."

He turned to face her more fully. "It makes no sense. Nonno never spoke of you to me, never said a word about having the art at the palazzo appraised before I left for Milan. I arrive home, and there you are."

"Your lack of communication is hardly my fault." That struck home, she thought, as she saw a vein begin to throb in his temple.

"We speak every day," he said with measured emphasis. "How could we not as we live in the same house."

"Easily, I should think, considering the size of the palazzo. It must be like living in a hotel with only two guests."

"Three, now that you've arrived."

"Lucky me. I get the room with the moss growing on the wall to match the green draperies."

"You can always go to a hotel if it's too damp for you," he said, a determined light in his eyes.

She had certainly walked into that one, not that it bothered her over much. "And miss the experience of a lifetime? I wouldn't think of it. Why, living in a palace is on everyone's bucket list."

"Palazzo," he corrected.

"Whatever." She waved that away with one hand.

"The palazzi of Venice are irreplaceable treasures."

"With price tags to match," she said with artless appreciation for their monetary value. It wouldn't do to disappoint him.

"So your countrymen discover when they decide to buy one after a visit or two. Not that it stops them."

She tipped her head in interest. "Someone on the plane said there are only 20,000 true Venetians who still own property in the city. Can that be true?"

He gave a short laugh. "It depends on who you ask. Those who collect taxes would say not, as Venetians are even less happy to pay taxes than your average Italian."

"Well, never mind. I can assure you I'm not looking for a permanent position of any kind, much less as mistress of the noble, but rather damp, pile you call home. I have a job to do. When it's over I'll be on my way."

He watched her, his gaze penetrating. It was an effort to sit still under that steady assessment when she knew what she'd just said in such earnest tones was a good deal less than the truth. But she could hardly explain without chancing being thrown out on her ear.

"*Bene*," he said with an abrupt nod. "I regret if I appeared less than welcoming. You will understand that I am concerned for my grandfather. He is of the old school, and so seldom sees anyone beyond family or friends that he can be easily taken in. And the palazzo's artwork is extremely valuable."

She sat up straight, clenching her hands in her lap. "Are you suggesting I have designs on it instead of—?"

"By no means."

"Good, because I can assure you I don't. Besides that, your grandfather doesn't strike me as a man who would be conned by just anyone."

"No, certainly not."

"Nor does he seem particularly innocent about human nature."

Lucca drew a deep breath that did interesting things to the fit of his suit coat over the broad width of his chest. "Signorina Steadman—"

"Celina," she said with a crooked smile. "Signorina Steadman seems a bit formal between two people who will be seeing a great deal of each other over the next few days."

~ ~ ~

A strand of her hair lay on the shoulder of her sweater, caught there by the beads braided into two small strands that clung to the knit fabric. Lucca's fingers itched with the need to pick up the bits of iridescent crystal and see how they were attached, to roll them between his fingers and maybe tug until she leaned toward him. She wouldn't expect that, he was sure. She'd be startled, her lips parting in protest or maybe with a question. He might manage to kiss her before she could make some snappy remark that would send his temper climbing.

He cursed silently as he realized the direction of his thoughts, embellishing the stringent phrases with all the artistry developed in Venice by Venetians who had, quite possibly, more to curse about than anyone else in Italy.

The last thing he needed to be thinking of just now was stealing a taste of this woman who had pushed her way into the Palazzo di Palladino. She might know a thing or two about art, but was no neutral expert whose interest was limited to paint and canvas, no mere cataloger of artists and eras and values. She was too intense, too interested in the old palazzo, too attentive toward his grandfather and, yes, even to him and what he had to say.

Not that she found him irresistible. He could almost think she saw him more as an impediment to whatever she wanted than as a man. She measured him, defied him, and taunted him. She was altogether too self-possessed and uncaring of how others saw her.

So he liked her enthusiasm for his city and found her candor and lack of pretense refreshing. So he felt some small curiosity about her life in the States and whether she had a romantic attachment there. So the merest brush of her arm or knee against him sent hot need zinging through him until his every nerve ending jangled in alarm. What did any of it matter against his gut instinct?

She was up to something; he could feel it.

His tactics with her just might have been all wrong to this point. He'd been thrown off balance by her sudden appearance, stirred against his will by moving in so close to her earlier there on her stepladder. If his nonno really had engaged her to appraise his artwork, she would not go quietly. He would have to find a way to make certain she caused no trouble.

Meanwhile, he needed to mend the impression he had given her. Not that he cared what she thought of him; it would simply be easier to keep tabs on what she was doing if she assumed he'd accepted having her around. He could watch at close range how she was progressing with the job she had been hired to complete, also how she was getting along with his grandfather.

The two of them, he and Celina Steadman, would be spending considerable time together, just as she had said. He would see it was not time wasted. And if the thought gave him greater satisfaction than was reasonable, that was something he chose to ignore.

From that moment, Lucca set out to be as pleasant as possible.

He apologized for the gray banks of clouds that moved in, turning everything dull and drear, but still pointed out the more famous landmarks of the city. He made certain she missed nothing of importance, from the stupendous palazzi of the Golden Crescent, where some of his most important work was being done, to the Bridge of Sighs, from San Giorgio Maggiore, floating like a dream upon the water as the afternoon turned misty, to the graceful yet substantial arch of the Rialto bridge, from various museums to the heart of Venice, the Campo di San Marco.

At the square, they docked and walked around a few minutes, but were soon driven into the shelter of a café by misting rain. Rather than more coffee on top of that they'd had earlier, they opted for gelato. Lucca expected Celina to choose something exotic, perhaps mango or pistachio, but she only asked for chocolate in a cone. With ice cream in hand, they sat watching the few winter tourists scurry across the square with a great flapping of their cheap plastic raincoats bought on the spot. Watched, too, a pair of policemen patrolling the edges with nonchalant strides, and red-legged pigeons avoiding the wet by waddling around beneath the tables under the café's awning.

Celina was quiet as she licked her way around her cone. Lucca watched her concentration, the flicker of her lashes as she gauged where to attack next, the delicate sweeps of her tongue. Something hot and insistent moved through him, settling in the pit of his stomach. He was suddenly aware of the pulse he could see beating in the hollow of her throat, of every breath that lifted the gentle curves beneath her sweater and the shimmer of raindrops in her hair that were almost a match for her entwined crystals.

Abruptly, she looked up. Her eyes, so blue before, seemed as gray as the day. There was a small smudge of chocolate on her bottom lip that she caught with a flick of her tongue. A faint rash of chill bumps beaded her forearms.

"Cold?" His cleared his throat to mask its unaccountable huskiness.

"Now why would you think that after ice cream on a winter's day?"

"We could have a coffee, after all." He glanced at her cone. "Or hot chocolate and a pastry."

She turned her attention to the canal that lay at the edge of the square. Black-painted gondolas covered with blue tarps, wet with rain, bobbed and weaved there with the wind-blown waves, along with their powerboat. "I'm fine," she answered, "but don't let that stop you."

"No." He dealt with a cold ooze of ice cream that threatened his fingers before glancing again at the boats and the gondolier who stood talking to Giovanni, their boatman. "You should take an evening gondola tour while you're here."

"Complete with serenade, I suppose."

"Why not? It's part of the experience."

"If you say so." Her tone was less than thrilled.

"You would be surprised how easy it is to imagine you are in the Venice of long ago, especially while traveling down the back canals. Some are so dark you'd think electricity hadn't been invented."

She gave him a swift upward glance. "I would never have taken you for a romantic."

"And you're not?"

"I didn't say that."

She hadn't, though he had a strong urge to make her admit to it. "I'm Italian," he said with a lifted shoulder. "What can you expect?"

"And you are always as expected, you do what's expected?"

"Often. Not always."

"Is that why we are having ice cream in St. Mark's Square?"

"*Gelato*," he corrected as her question almost triggered his smile. "Of course, what you need for the full effect is to come here at midnight to stroll the square under a full moon."

"Right," she drawled.

"People who aren't romantics miss a lot of pleasure in life. To avoid something merely because it sounds corny or touristy is foolish."

"Or simply practical, if it isn't worth the effort."

"You'll never find out unless you try. Besides, one person may notice bird droppings on the cobblestones and flood waters creeping toward them out of the canal—but another will see the silver shimmer of moonlight as it has fallen on this place for a thousand years."

She watched him a long moment with something like bemusement in her eyes. Then her lashes came down. "But the reality will still be that the water is rising."

"*Certo.* And too much attention to reality can be deadly dull."

"Yet you're the one who's trying to keep Venice from drowning in the sea."

"Slowing it down as much as possible," he corrected with wry fatalism. "It's been sinking at a rate of an inch and a half per century for hundreds of years, or so statistics tell us, though the process seems to be gathering speed. More than that, we are told it is slowly moving eastward out to sea, as if it means to hurry its burial."

"Now there's a comforting thought," she protested with a frown.

"Meanwhile, millions of euros have been spent to build a system of movable dams around the city. The project has taken decades, is now being called finished for all rights and purposes, though who knows when or if it will ever be really done. But with any luck, it will be centuries before Venice becomes a mecca for deep sea divers."

"But why try if the end is inevitable?"

"Many things can happen to avert an unwelcome fate."

She smiled at that, a rueful curving of her lips. "My grandmother used to say the same thing."

So had his grandfather, which was where he had gotten the saying, now that he thought of it. "Used to? Does that mean she's gone?"

"Two years ago this month. Cancer."

"I'm sorry. I didn't quite realize, though I know Massimo said you were restoring the cottage that belonged to her."

"She left it to me because she knew how much it meant to me, and how little my father cared for it." Her smile wobbled at the edges as it faded.

The need to keep her talking, to learn more of what she felt and thought, was too strong to resist. "And her paintings, since she was an artist?"

"Mine as well. My father would probably have burned everything."

"I take it he had no appreciation."

"Not for her paintings, and even less for art in general. He doesn't care for much other than work or getting ahead, if it comes to that. He is very like his father, my grandfather, was, that way."

Lucca tried to picture his own grandfather in that light but failed. Nonno was interested in so many things, had a deep and abiding love of all that was beautiful and uplifting to the heart even when it was fundamentally useless. That he was very like him was a given. And though it troubled him to consider it, he felt Celina might also be more like her artistic grandmother than not.

"Yet she painted, your grandmother, and you made your profession in the art world. It must have been a struggle for both of you to make that happen."

An expression too fleeting for recognition came and went across her face. "You could say that." Rising from her chair with an abrupt movement, she discarded what was left of her cone in a nearby trash can, wiped her hands on her napkin and tossed that as well. "We should go back, don't you think? I'm sure you have work waiting for you."

Lucca did, indeed, but was in no special hurry to return to it. It was amazing how little he cared about work at that particular moment.

Chapter Three

"You enjoyed your outing? My grandson gave you the—how do you say?—the grand tour?"

Massimo folded the newspaper he was reading and put it aside as Celina came into the salon. He sat in a wingback chair covered in faded damask before the fire that burned in cheery brightness beneath a mantel of carved marble. The glow from a lamp on the table beside him offset the dimness caused by the day's gloom. It appeared he was waiting for her return, Celina thought, but surely that could not be right?

"Absolutely," she answered with a smile. "Thank you so much for suggesting it."

"Lucca did not return with you, I see."

"He said something about checking with his office, I believe."

"Yes, of course, always the work. But no matter. You will

perhaps be more comfortable in Venice now, with a better idea of where you are and how the city lies around you. You noticed our fine islands, Murano, Burano and Torcello, yes? You now know what else you might like to see?"

"I did and I do, though I'm not here to play tourist."

"Nor are you here to slave away all day," he said with a flick of his fingers for such a thought. "Nothing and no one requires it. You must not allow Lucca to make you feel the need."

"No, I won't do that."

Even as she spoke, her thoughts returned to the boat tour and the man who had been her guide. She couldn't say the time spent with him had been especially comfortable, but it had been enlightening. How many of the men she knew could claim to be a romantic without blushing? And yet Lucca managed it with no loss whatever of his macho assurance.

He was suspicious where she was concerned, yes, but the man was also seriously hot. He was strong as well, with plenty of muscle beneath his expensive suit. And yet the hard cast of his features softened when he spoke of his grandfather. His sense of humor was subtle, yet gleamed bright in his eyes. He had real affection for the city of his birth, also passion for its welfare that he didn't mind showing. She'd never met a man quite like him.

"My grandson means nothing by his frowns, you understand. He's a good man, a generous man, though sometimes heavy-handed in his care for me." Massimo's voice turned dry. "He forgets I have looked after my affairs without his help these many years, and shall for a few more."

"It's nice of him to be concerned." She meant that, in all truth. She had felt much the same about her grandmother.

"The two of you came to agreement, then?"

"I suppose." It was more on the order of a truce, but there was no need to trouble her host with it.

"Excellent." Massimo pushed to his feet, moving to where a drinks tray sat on a side table. "Will you have a sherry to warm you after your outing?"

Celina nodded, as she was a little chilled. At the same time, she had to smile. Coffee, biscotti, gelato and now sherry? She could get used to what seemed to be an Italian habit of plying people with food and drink.

"I see you found the ladder Sergio brought up for you." Massimo, pouring wine into two glasses, tipped his head toward where it still sat beneath the portrait of the late Conte Lucca di Palladino.

"I did, yes, thank you."

"It appears none too steady. I believe it must be replaced."

"It's fine, really," she said, accepting the glass he handed her. "Don't go to any extra trouble."

"I could not live with myself if you fell and were seriously injured. You will do me the favor of avoiding it for now, if you please. Besides, tomorrow is time enough for serious work."

"Oh, but—"

"For now, I thought to show you more of the palazzo. Drink your sherry, then I will give myself the pleasure of pointing out some of my favorite canvases and telling you their stories."

"Lovely," she said with anticipation lilting in her voice. "Nothing could suit me better."

The palazzo was a treasure house; there was no other word for it. The late conte's portrait she had already inspected in the salon turned out to be by Moroni, and two others were by Savoldo and Veronese. The dining room held a large Tintoretto, a back sitting room was graced by a Titian, and a long gallery with tall windows overlooking a side canal was lined with a whole series by Canaletto.

"And this room," Massimo said as he opened the door and ushered Celina inside, "was favored by my late wife. She was French, at least on her mother's side, and preferred more modern artists."

That was true only in relation to the rest of the house, Celina saw at once. A stunning cubist work from Csaky was centered above a bed that looked like something from a Thirties movie, sleek yet stark. The rug that centered the wood floor featured geometric lines inset with earth colors against a muddy cream ground, very Art Deco, and a set of four lithographs on a side wall were in a similar style. The impression was not of décor lingering from the 1930s, however, but rather of a heavy-handed attempt to recreate it.

"Interesting," she murmured in neutral tones.

"Vapid," Massimo said with a grimace, "but she tired of what she called the decadent grandeur of Venice, and this was the result. I should change it, but it's easier to just shut the door upon it."

It sounded as if he'd shut away the memory of his wife as well. Perhaps he had, for there was no sign the room had ever been occupied by a couple, no door that might connect to a master bedroom.

"But you would like the pieces in here valued as well?" Celina asked.

"If you will."

"I don't want to intrude. Maybe they could be moved somewhere else for inspection."

"It will be no intrusion, I promise you. My wife passed away a few months ago, though she'd been ill for years. She enjoyed company, and would not mind that you are here."

She had not known when his wife died. It changed nothing that he had not been a widower for long, but she felt the easing of a small tightness somewhere in the back of her mind. "If you're sure."

"*Certo*, quite sure." He turned off the lights and stood aside while she left the room, then closed the door behind them. In the hall outside, he paused for a moment in the evening's gloom that had deepened as they made their round. "Forgive me, signorina, but—"

"Celina, please. Signorina seems so formal." Having extended that favor to Lucca, she should certainly do the same for her employer.

"Only if you call me Massimo," he answered, with a small, courtly bow.

"An odd name, one I'd never heard before I saw it on your email."

"Odd in the States, it may be, but not here. It's from the

Latin Maximus."

"Now that makes perfect sense." The smile she turned upon him was warm, there in the long corridor that was almost dark but for the light falling through a long window at the far end. "But you were saying?"

"I only meant to tell you ... that is to say, when I look at you, I am reminded of someone I knew long ago."

"Are you?" She waited, her heart thudding uncomfortably in her chest. His face was hard to make out in the dimness.

"She was American also." He shook his head. "That may be the reason."

"You knew her here in Venice?"

"Oh, yes. I've never been to the States."

That seemed a sad admission, or maybe she only wanted to hear it that way. She forced lightness into her voice as spoke. "A holiday romance, no doubt?"

"You could call it that."

"It didn't work out," she suggested in soft inquiry. It almost seemed he'd been disappointed in her comment, but that was unlikely. Wasn't it?

A shadow crossed his face, part regret, part anguish, part wry resignation, before he turned back to her. "It was a long time ago, before I married." He made a smooth, dismissive gesture before indicating the hall ahead of them. "Allow me to show you another room or two."

Celina would have liked to pursue the subject, but didn't want to push too hard or too fast. She moved ahead of him in search of more painted treasures.

Lucca appeared again in time for dinner. It was served in the formal dining room, complete with candlelight that brought out the colors in the Tintoretto, and gleamed in the heavy silver and ornate crystal of the place settings. They began with seafood pasta, continued with veal and a vegetable medley, and ended with a cream cake rich with chopped nuts and bits of orange zest.

Massimo sat at the head of the table with Celina on his right and Lucca across from her, on his grandfather's left. Conversation was in English in deference to Celina as a guest, and ranged from one subject to another at Massimo's direction, from politics and a recent art auction in the city to comparisons between the carnival seasons in Rio, New Orleans and Venice.

"It occurs to me," her host said, as he leaned back in his chair, a small glass of dessert liqueur in his hand, "that a party is in order, a gathering in honor of *carnevale*. What say you, Lucca?"

"If you like." His grandson surveyed him, his dark gaze intent, as if searching for the meaning behind the suggestion.

"I do like. In costume, of course."

"Oh, of course."

Massimo ignored the dry note in his grandson's voice. "If the date is set for eight days from now, we will be able to go on to the Toso ball afterwards. My good friend will be more than happy to welcome any guest we care to bring."

"Oh, no, not if you mean me," Celina said at once. "I didn't come prepared for anything so grand sounding as that." She was far more aware of the glance Lucca settled upon her than she wanted to be. It had a brooding intensity that set her pulse to racing. The play of candlelight over the striking planes and hollows of his face, the golden glint of it in the darkness of his eyes, stole the breath from her lungs.

Massimo's eyes crinkled at the corners as he smiled. "This is not a problem, as you say in the States. Because it is my wish and my pleasure, everything shall be supplied for you."

"I can't let you do that. Besides, I wouldn't know anyone, don't really know the language." She'd studied Italian in college, often spoke a few words with her grandmother who had picked it up while in Venice years before, but that hardly made her fluent.

"You will know me and you will know Lucca," Massimo answered with grand disregard for her misgivings. "Once you arrive in our company, everyone will know you."

Celina could not prevent a low laugh for the sublime arrogance behind that idea. "Will they, now?"

"There is not a doubt of it." He reached to touch the back of her left hand she was using to steady her plate while she cut a bite of cake. Humor was bright in the faded brown of his eyes. "It has been some little time since I escorted a lovely young lady. Will you not consent so I may live those days again?"

"Well, the party may be okay." She could almost feel her resolve melting away under his benevolent gaze.

"But yes, you must have this experience of a *carnevale* ball as well while you are here. Already, my mind busies itself with the costume that will best become you."

He seemed so pleased at the prospect that Celina could argue no farther. She should insist on finding her own costume, regardless, but hardly knew where to look, much less what would be appropriate. Anyway, how much trouble could a simple costume be? She turned her wrist, clasping his hand. "All right, but please, nothing too far out."

"Nothing far out at all," he answered with promise in his voice and the flash of humor in his face. "You will be stunning, absolutely beautiful. How could it be otherwise?"

She laughed again at his droll flattery, but couldn't help being warmed by it. She could get used to such forthright admiration, even if it wasn't deserved.

~ ~ ~

Lucca pushed his plate away as his appetite deserted him. Taking up his espresso, he spooned sugar into it, stirring while he watched Celina.

For all the attention she had paid him throughout this dinner, he might as well not have been there. She and his grandfather were complete in and of themselves. Nonno was holding her hand now, smiling upon her as if he had known her in her cradle instead of only meeting her less than two days ago.

What had come over him?

He could not accuse Celina of being deliberately enticing. She was pleasant, answering whatever was put to her, keeping up her end of the dinner table conversation without holding the floor. She was not coquettish or flirtatious in any way.

And yet... Something nagged at him.

Did she hold his grandfather's hand a little longer than was strictly necessary? Was it his imagination, or did she study him from the corners of her eyes when he turned away from her?

Dio, but it was annoying. He was not used to women who paid more attention to his septuagenarian grandfather than to him.

Not that he was jealous, certainly not. That would be too ridiculous.

He was uneasy, that was it. Men like his nonno had been known to go off the deep end after regaining their freedom following the death of a wife. They often married the first attractive female to cross their path, particularly if she was young and nubile and smart enough to appear flattered by their attention.

It would be understandable, too, for Nonno—at least to a point. Everyone knew the woman he'd married was less than perfect as a wife, mother or grandmother. Ill health had been her hobby, and she complained endlessly of her aches and pains in a high-pitched voice as grating as the whine of a mosquito. Demanding one moment and martyred the next, she controlled everything in her orbit, limited though that might be by the fact that she seldom left her bed. It was complications from diabetes that carried her off finally, complications that came about because she was too self-indulgent to follow the restricted diet that might have kept the disease under control.

Still, she had loved his grandfather in her way. Lucca sometimes thought she might have been a better wife if she had loved him less. She had longed for blind, passionate devotion. When it was not forthcoming, she turned needy yet vindictive in her disappointment. Her bad health had begun as an unconscious means of preventing her husband from leaving her, but ended being the thing that finally set him free.

Nonno had been an exemplary husband to the bitter end, as everyone knew, faithful, kind and unfailingly polite. He deserved a little happiness to go with his freedom. Nevertheless, an irresponsible affair with a young woman a third his age seemed the wrong way to find it. Add the possibility that Celina Steadman might have an agenda, and it was unlikely any good could come of this business.

She was young and brimming with health and vitality, lovely and somehow unspoiled. How could his grandfather not want to possess all that energy, the delectable body with its firm curves and skin so fine it begged to be touch? Celina was not yet aware of how easily she could attract a man of nonno's age and outlook, Lucca was almost sure. Yet the way things were going, it would not be long before she figured it out.

What then?

Lucca could see only one way to prevent this disaster in the making. The question was whether his grandfather would recognize it as being for his good, or forgive him if he succeeded.

"Shall we take our coffee to the salon?" he asked in

abrupt decision. "The fire there should have taken more of the dampness from the air."

"A fine suggestion," Nonno said at once. "Bring Celina's cup, will you, Lucca?"

The wily old fox. While he helped Celina with her heavy chair and gave her his arm, Lucca was left to bring up the rear. He might have laughed if he hadn't been so exasperated. At least he was saved from having his hands full of cups and saucers. It was Sergio who gathered them on a tray and followed them into the salon.

Lucca skirted the sofa that faced the fireplace, at right angles to the pair of wingback armchairs on either side. Waiting until Nonno seated Celina on it, he slid in next to her, leaving his grandfather to take a different seat.

Massimo gave him a frown. Lucca returned it with a look of bland inquiry while waiting for Sergio to set out their espressos and vanish back toward the kitchen. Then he turned to their guest.

"You have a time frame for the appraisal you'll be doing here?" he asked. "In other words, how long will we enjoy your company?"

"I can't really say until I've looked over the full collection," she answered, her expression guarded as she met his gaze. "Most of yesterday was spent settling in, though I saw more this afternoon."

"Did you?" Lucca heard the tightness in his voice, but couldn't prevent it.

"Only a portion," Nonno answered for her, "the major works in the main rooms." He took a sip from the cup in his hand as he relaxed, stretching one elegantly shod foot toward the fire. "It seemed best not to frighten her away by showing her the whole."

"Wise decision," Lucca said smoothly without taking his gaze from Celina. "You do know there are more than forty rooms?"

"Wow." The curves of her mouth tilted at one corner. "I knew the place was big, but not that big."

"And what do you think so far?" The question was a ploy to retain her attention, but he was interested in the answer as well.

"I'm impressed beyond words. If the rest have the same riches as those I've seen, the job may take a while."

"Let us hope," Lucca said at once, smiling into her eyes.

Celina's face went blank. He could almost feel her withdrawal. She was bright enough to realize some purpose lay behind his questions, and was not going to make things easy for him. He was hardly surprised when she turned away from him.

"I don't believe you ever said why you were having an appraisal done," she said to Nonno. "Did you have in mind putting them up for auction?"

"At the house where you work, perhaps?" He lifted a shoulder in an apologetic shrug. "You will forgive me, but no."

"What then? To value them as part of your estate?" Her face changed. "You don't intend to donate them to a museum, surely?"

"Neither of those things, as it happens." Nonno sent

Lucca a quick glance. "Given the number of times I've been told the palazzo is about to topple into the sea, it seemed a good idea to finally insure what is inside it."

Celina's eyes widened. Some of the color receded from her face. "You mean ... you're saying they aren't insured now?"

"It's always been here, this artwork, most of it, anyway." Nonno gestured with one hand. "It seemed it always would be here."

Lucca had not known. It had never occurred to him to ask. He felt a little lightheaded at the thought of the loss should a fire break out or storm surge bring higher water than they'd had in the past. He couldn't even begin to feature the loss should thieves decide to make the palazzo a target.

There was no alarm system, of course. His grandfather had little patience with technology, in spite of the computer in his study. He often declared that whatever had been good enough for his ancestors who had lived and died on the Grand Canal was good enough for him.

"You've had no insurance all this time?" Lucca asked in slow disbelief. "Not when my father set off Roman candles from the loggia and accidentally caught the window draperies on fire? Not when my friends and I chased each other up and down the rooms with water pistols, shooting at everything that didn't move."

"You did no great damage," Massimo said with a smile of fond remembrance.

"We could have lowered the value of things by several

hundred thousand euros. I remember shooting the old conte over there in the eye myself." Lucca glanced at his ancestor, but the figure in the painting only smiled the same enigmatic yet forbearing smile he always had.

"It's oil on canvas. A little water wasn't going to hurt it, especially when there were plenty of people around to dry it again."

Celina had been following the exchange with concern in the blue depths of her eyes. Now she sprang to her feet and walked to where the portrait hung. Stepping close, she stood frowning up at the face of the long dead conte.

Lucca rose to follow her without a second thought. Stopping at her shoulder, he tracked her gaze. The conte stared down at them as if waiting for their verdict on how he'd survived the indignity of being shot with a water pistol.

"See anything that needs repair?" Lucca asked after a moment. He could sense the warmth of her body so close to his, catch the tantalizing, sun-ripe peach base note of the perfume she wore, one so delectable that it made him want to peel off her clothes and taste her skin, inch by warm inch.

"Not from this far away. I noticed nothing this morning while closer, either."

"You see," Massimo put in from behind them with great satisfaction in his voice. "I'd like to see a thief walk off with that piece, anyway. He'd have problems just getting it through the door."

"Not if he cut it from its frame and rolled it," Celina said quietly.

Lucca winced; he couldn't help it. "The paints wouldn't

hold up under that, not after all this time."

"Not his problem if it cracks and falls off in layers."

She was right, not that he intended to admit it. "It seems, then," he said evenly, "the sooner you get your job done, the better it will be."

She sent him a quick upward glance, as if she could read the subtext of what he said without half trying. "It does, doesn't it?"

The trouble for Lucca was that this subtext, which was that the sooner she was done, the better, suddenly seemed all wrong.

A short time later, Celina excused herself and left them to go in search of her room. She was a little tired, she said, probably the last remnants of jet lag from her long flight over.

Lucca was forced to wonder if it was to avoid him. Regardless, he walked with her to the foot of the staircase that rose from one end of the salon as an act of simple courtesy. She didn't seem to appreciate it for she slanted a frown at him before turning to climb the marble treads.

He stood quite still, his gaze intent as he watched her move upward with light, athletic steps. He could not look away from the straightness of her spine, the sway of her hips or the smooth movement of the muscles in her legs. It was a long moment before he realized his grandfather had come to stand beside him.

"Well?"

Lucca controlled his start before he half turned to glance at him. "Well what?"

"To have you with us for dinner was an unexpected pleasure, given your usual work schedule. You needn't tell me the cause was not our house guest."

"No, I won't do that."

"She is delightful, beyond a doubt, but hardly your type."

Nonno paused, as if waiting for him to comment. Lucca obliged him. "I wasn't aware I had a type."

"Sophisticated women, usually, those who expect little from you beyond courtesy, flowers, and the occasional gift of jewelry. Oh yes, and a pleasurable time."

His grandfather paid more attention to his affairs than he'd realized. It was something to remember. "She's hardly your type, either," he said, his voice even.

"Which is as well, as I have no designs upon her."

Relief loosened Lucca's breathing. He pulled air deeper into his lungs. "You don't?"

"I don't. What I want to know is what you're about."

"You're asking my intentions? A bit Victorian even for you, isn't it?"

No answering amusement lighted Nonno's face. "Celina is a guest in my house."

"She is an appraiser being paid to do a job."

"I am responsible for her welfare while she is here."

Lucca swung to face him. "*Dio*, you sound as if you think I mean to attack her as she sleeps! She's attractive, interesting, and definitely sexy in a long-legged American fashion. Can't I just be attracted to her?"

"You could, but I don't think that's it." His grandfather's eyes narrowed. "What are you about?"

"What if I said a little light seduction? Would that be so bad?"

Nonno straightened to his full height. "You cannot be serious!"

"You need not worry. If she loves you, she won't be tempted, and if she doesn't and is tempted, then you're better off knowing it."

"Don't be insulting."

That tone, so laden with disappointment beneath its anger, told Lucca he'd gone too far. He forced a laugh. "Of course not. I was only joking. Your Celina is safe from me."

His grandfather did not relax. "So I should hope. I will have nothing less than the greatest respect shown toward Signorina Steadman."

It was a warning. And the quiet power of it was more disturbing to Lucca than all the curses ever heard in Venice. It meant the situation with Nonno was serious, far more so than he'd expected. It might even be too serious to be mended.

The only solution he could see was to prove to him Celina was not as innocent as he thought, or as free of guilty intentions.

Chapter Four

Celina rolled out of bed early. She was a morning person, but mainly she couldn't wait to get started. She did love her job. Paint and canvas, line, color, shadow, brush strokes—everything about it fascinated her.

She'd tried her hand at painting, using watercolor techniques for mixed media. She'd enjoyed the experiment, learned much from it, but soon realized she lacked the eye for detail shown by her grandmother, not to mention the dedication. Studying art and artists, absorbing their wonderfully different styles, their juxtaposition of colors for tension or harmony, satisfied her just as well.

She was halfway to the en suite bathroom when she heard singing. The voice was a mellow baritone, and the song so familiar, so perfect for its setting that she gave a low laugh.

Grabbing her robe that lay across the foot of the bed, she

pulled it on as she turned to the French doors that gave onto a balcony overlooking a secondary canal. She jerked the belt tied, ducked between the draperies and pushed outside.

The singer was a gondolier, just as she expected. He was coming toward her with slow sweeps of his oar, nattily dressed in the black-and-white striped shirt and black pants of his calling. His gondola, painted shining black with an upright and curved prow and red velvet seats, was empty, so he was alone as he belted out *O Sole Mio*. His song about sunshine had to be a joke, however, for he was getting wet. A light rain was falling, dimpling the milky green surface of the canal, also splattering onto the balcony where she stood before dripping back into the water below.

Delighted appreciation rose inside her. Bringing her hands together, she began to applaud.

The gondolier looked up with a cheery grin and quick inclination of his dark, curly head that was spangled with raindrops. "*Grazie, signorina bella! Buon giorno!*"

"Good morning," she returned, and watched, smiling, as he saluted but kept going on whatever mission he had underway, moving swiftly out of sight around a bend.

"Good morning to you, too."

The greeting came from another small balcony just down from where she stood. She swung her head to see Lucca, dressed more casually this morning in pressed jeans and a sweater in muted earth and sky tones. He stood with his hands braced on his balcony railing, looking far too competent and alert for someone who had not yet had his morning coffee.

"*Buon giorno.*" She clasped the opening of her robe with one hand while raking back her hair with the other. She was suddenly aware of the cold and wet floor of the balcony under her bare feet.

A brief smile lighted his face, though it faded as he nodded toward where the gondolier had disappeared. "I would not encourage that one, were I you. Men like him have an excellent memory for places, and the water level is not that far below where you stand."

She stared at him while the rain spattered around them and ran with a musical trickle down a gutter somewhere nearby. "Are you saying—?"

"You might also make certain your door is locked."

"Oh, please. That's just too, too—"

"Too Italian, you'd say? How else do you think balcony access to a lady's bedroom became such a cliché?"

She crossed her arms over her chest while still frowning at him. "A man going to such lengths would have to be sure of his welcome."

"Or suspect it." His gaze traveled without haste from her tousled hair and short travel robe down her bare legs that were now pebbled with goose bumps. Not all of them from cold.

"Are you suggesting I might let him in?"

He gave a considered shake of his head. "Only that it could look that way if he wanted to be optimistic."

She opened her mouth to blast him, but could find no words. Meanwhile, the rain quickened, coming down hard enough to dampen her shoulders and the tops of her breasts where her arms pushed them together. A shiver caught her as she saw him follow her gaze with his own.

Swinging with the abruptness of anger, she almost slipped in the water pooling on the balcony floor. She caught herself with no damage except to her dignity. Stepping inside, she closed the French door with a bang and jerked the draperies tight across them.

Celina showered in record time, muttering all the while about know-it-all Venetian men. With a grim smile for the irony of it, and the defiance, she pulled on a sweater with wide horizontal stripes in black and white that was not unlike the gondolier's, and then stepped into black knit pants. She'd pulled the beads from her hair the night before, and this morning she simply pushed it back out of her face with a black bandeau. Leaving off makeup, as she would be working in the depths of this cavernous old palazzo all day, she went in search of breakfast.

Sergio gave her coffee and rolls with butter and strawberry jam. Signor Lucca had gone already, so the manservant said, and Signor Massimo was not up yet. No instructions had been left for the signorina, no message except she was not to be hindered in any way, but allowed free run of the house. She must do as she pleased.

What pleased Celina was taking her second cup of coffee into the salon and drinking it while she stared up at the old conte in his heavy frame. The more she looked at him, the more she saw Lucca in his every feature. The main difference was an elusive softness that the artist has caught in the eyes of the portrait, half-hidden behind the devilish hint of humor. She'd seen that only once in Massimo's grandson, there in St. Mark's Square when he spoke of being a romantic.

It seemed unlikely she would see it again, not while he distrusted her reasons for being there. That he was right made no difference. It still bothered her.

He'd unbent a little more after dinner the night before. It was a nice change. The trouble was, she didn't quite believe in his switch from suspicion to flirtation. Oh, he'd shown a certain awareness of her before, but that had not kept him from making her feel about as welcome as a seagull at a fish market.

This morning on the balcony he was back to being insulting again. Well, more or less. She should be flattered, she supposed, that he thought her attractive enough to entice men to swarm up to her balcony. That didn't keep her from being incensed at his hint she might let them in. Though she might, at that, if they looked like the long-departed first Conte Lucca di Palladino.

She sighed a little, her gaze on the nobleman above her. Too bad his great-great-however-many grandson wasn't more like him. Not that it mattered. She was here to do a job. She would complete it in due time, discover what she'd come to find out, and then she'd be gone. The modern Lucca Palladino had nothing to do with it, nothing at all.

Draining her coffee cup, she carried it back to the dining room. She picked up her briefcase brought down earlier that held all her supplies and set to work.

A feature of the palazzo's second floor was a library. Lined floor to ceiling with bookshelves, some of which could only be reached by a rolling ladder, it opened onto a back loggia not unlike the one which fronted the huge old building. The heavy draperies at the French doors had been pulled open, allowing the wavering light reflections caused by the morning's dim and watery sunlight on the water to penetrate the room.

That the library served as Massimo's office seemed clear from the great, heavy desk which anchored one end of the space, along with wooden file cabinets with time-worn brass handles. A cutting-edge desktop computer held pride of place on the desk, along with a litter of papers, books left lying face-down to mark their pages and a collection of notes on everything from a train ticket stub to a wine coaster.

The desk drew Celina like a magnet. She circled it, squinting to read what appeared to be invoices and clippings, computer printouts and calendars. She was just reaching to pick up a printed list when she heard the creak of an uneven floorboard in the hall outside. She reached quickly for a pen that lay close to hand.

"What are you doing in here?"

She'd known it would be Lucca from the sound of his footsteps. She startled anyway, turning quickly at the deep sound of his voice. That didn't keep her from waggling the pen at him by way of answer for his question.

"You won't find any artwork in here." He gestured around him. "No free walls for it."

"I did notice," she said, her voice dry. Let him think what he pleased. She wasn't about to admit to snooping.

"Was there something else you needed from my desk?"

"Yours?"

She looked up from jotting a quick note in the notebook she'd taken from her briefcase. She could feel her face grow hot, though why she should be embarrassed at invading his office instead of Massimo's was hard to say. "I thought you worked in the city center somewhere. In fact, Sergio said you'd gone already."

"I had," he answered. "But it seemed a good idea to resume work on the palazzo for now, or at least shore up the *fondamenta*, the walkway, in front of it."

That was nothing more than a thinly veiled excuse to keep an eye on her, Celina was almost sure. At least he was being polite about it. The best thing she could do for now was pretend to believe him. "There's danger of flooding?"

"Always, at this time of year. They don't call it the season of *acqua alta* for nothing."

Acqua alta, high water, she translated in silent bemusement as she met his dark gaze. It sounded ominous somehow.

He looked entirely too good in his designer jeans and beautifully knitted sweater with the sleeves pushed to the elbows, exposing firmly muscled forearms sprinkled with dark hair. She was reminded more vividly than she liked of their early-morning balcony meeting. It didn't help to see his gaze linger on her gondolier's sweater, or the tug of a smile at the corner of his mouth as he apparently recognized the defiant impulse behind it.

"Must be nice to do whatever you like whenever you take the notion," she said in dry appreciation.

"One of the perks of independent wealth." Moving into the room, he seated himself on the corner of the desk with one foot on the floor. Without being conspicuous about it, she had to admit, he glanced over the littered surface to see what might have interested her.

"Lucky you."

It wasn't exactly news that he was well off. Beyond the obvious grandeur of the house, Massimo and his grandson were looked after by a staff of eight or so. There was a chef and his two helpers, a maid for each floor, and a general handyman who seemed to be kept busy with maintenance inside and out. This was in addition to Sergio and Giovanni, who handled the private powerboat.

"Credit my grandmother," Lucca said easily. "The Palladinos have never been paupers, but what she brought to her marriage with Nonno multiplied their net worth many times over."

She lifted a brow. "You make it sound like some old-fashioned dowry arrangement."

"Not quite," he answered with a low laugh. "She was an heiress, that's all."

"So the palazzo is safe for one more generation."

"And another beyond that. Being her only grandchild, as well as her favorite, she left the bulk of her estate to me, just as yours left hers to you."

"Instead of to Massimo?" she asked in surprise.

"He has use of it, but that's all. Not that he cares as long as life at the palazzo doesn't change. And he is aware, of course, that I'll have need of it when the title falls to me."

She gave him her full attention then. "You'll be the next Conte di Palladino."

"Since my father was an only child and died when I was a child." He inclined his head in token of agreement.

"Both wealthy and titled. How nice for you."

"If it sounds a bit arrogant, I apologize," he said, his teeth gleaming white in his tanned face as he flashed his charming smile. "I thought you might find the family history interesting. Are you sure you don't want to hear how the first Conte Lucca earned his title as a merchant prince? Or how Massimo's father dabbled in tourism after the Second World War, built an empire on the tourist trade, and helped make Venice one of the top ten destinations in the world? Yes, and how some of the mechanical processes which I pioneered and developed for saving Venice are now used worldwide?"

"So you profited to the tune of millions, I suppose?"

"Give or take a few zeros."

It was billions, then. She might have known.

He sat there, relaxed and confident of his place in the world and ability to control it. And his expression was such an exact copy of that on his ancestor in the painting downstairs that it was almost uncanny. Why that was especially alluring, she could not say, except that it had nothing to do with zeros or euros. Nor could she tell why the fact she felt that way should be so irritating. "It didn't occur to you to provide your innovations for the benefit of mankind?"

"That isn't the way of the world." He lifted a broad shoulder. "If I had not taken ownership of the discoveries, someone else would have."

What he said was undoubtedly true, which meant she was being unfair. It wasn't like her. She was usually more than reasonable.

This whole business had her nerves on edge. It was the uncertainty of it, she knew, as well as the deception and growing fear of what she might discover.

Why she was afraid was something else she preferred not to think about, not until it became absolutely necessary.

"And I should be interested because?"

He swung his foot where his leg was propped on the desk, watching her with dark eyes alight with amusement. "Don't tell me you haven't thought of writing about the collection, maybe some scholarly article for the magazine published by your auction house? You'll need local color, family details, provenance for any paintings you include. I'm surprised you don't have a camera with you for recording details you might want later."

"I'd intended asking Massimo about photos."

"Why bother? It's clear he'll deny you nothing."

She chose to misunderstand him. "He's been extremely accommodating, but I doubt he'll be okay with anything he thinks might be damaging."

"And I doubt he'll object if you ask nicely enough." He watched her with such intensity in the coffee blackness of his eyes that her skin prickled where his gaze touched.

"If you are suggesting..."

"What?" he asked, easing off the desk and strolling toward her as she came to a halt.

To retreat would only make him bolder, she thought. Yet standing her ground wasn't easy. He was tall and hard-muscled, carrying inner strength she recognized even before he was close enough that she could feel the warmth of his body, catch the tantalizing scent of the men's fragrance he wore.

"Massimo is my employer, nothing more," she said with every ounce of firmness she could command. "To suggest anything else is ridiculous."

"But you don't call him Signor Palladino."

"Well, no, but—"

"But what?" he took her up at once. "Which one of you established this relationship that has become so cozy so quickly? If not you, what do you expect to gain from letting it happen?"

"I don't know what you're talking about."

He reached to touch her cheek with his knuckle, sliding it over the turn of her jaw to her neck where her pulse beat with a hard, fast rhythm. The trail he made brought her nerve endings to tingling life, like a thousand tiny firecrackers going off beneath the skin.

She stepped back, spun away from him. Even as she moved, he reached out to catch her wrist. She came to a halt, but refused to give him the satisfaction of struggling in his grasp. The effort of self-control left her breathless with anger and barely suppressed urges she refused to acknowledge.

"If it's an Italian fling you want, *cara*," he said in a voice like warm velvet, "I can also accommodate you. Nothing against my grandfather, but I believe you would find it more—satisfying."

"*Do* you now?"

"I promise it."

Those three words were vibrant with sincerity. She believed them, she really did, but that didn't make the idea any less insulting.

Leaning toward him, she allowed a husky note to invade her own voice. "Tempting. Very tempting."

"*Cara*." His gaze settled on her mouth. He eased closer until she could feel the heated hardness of his leg muscles, and something else, brush her thigh. She went perfectly still, half mesmerized by the pure masculine force of him that surrounded her. She watched his mouth ease closer until her eyelids drifted shut.

His mouth touched hers, smooth, warm, exquisitely tender. Her lips throbbed with her heartbeat, burning where the surfaces came together, softening until they molded to his. She caught the faintest hint of his sweet taste, the rasp of the beard stubble at the corner of his mouth. Her strength seemed to be draining away, so she wanted to press against him, hold on to him, absorbing his power and promise.

This would not do. It would not do at all.

Jerking free of his hold, she backed away until there was a good six feet between them. "Or it might be tempting," she said in tight disdain, "if I was some empty-headed teenager full of raging hormones and sexy intentions while away from the States for the first time. As it is, I have a job to do and no time to waste."

"What makes you think the time would be wasted?" A glaze of color appeared on his face and neck, while something hot and daring burned with fiery purpose in the depths of his eyes.

She didn't, actually. She could feel warmth in her own face, was aware of the swift rise and fall of her breathing and tight contraction of her nipples under her concealing sweater. The time might come when she would be sorry she had passed up the chance of a hot affair with an Italian like Lucca Palladino. But she wasn't going to be treated like some mindless opportunist who could be distracted by sex, no matter how *satisfying* it might promise to be.

On the other hand, she didn't want to make an enemy of him. It would be far better to have him on her side. She might not want to embark on an affair that could end in her getting hurt, but she could at least try to get along with him.

"Look," she said, keeping her voice even with an effort, "I don't know what you think is going on, but I have no designs on your grandfather. He's a nice man, a gentleman of the old school, and I like him a lot, but that's as far as it goes. I'm here to look at his artwork, but even if I had something else on my mind, I feel sure it would be useless. Massimo doesn't strike me as the kind of man who needs arm candy my age to massage his ego."

Lucca watched her for unblinking seconds before

shaking his head. "Ah no, *cara*, all men are that kind if the moment is right, and the woman."

"You would know, I suppose."

"You may trust me on this if on nothing else."

"Well, I'm not interested, so you can stop worrying. Now if you'll excuse me, I have work to do." Swinging away from him again, she marched from the library. She didn't slam the door behind her, but that was only because it was standing open and she had no need to shut it.

~ ~ ~

That did not go well.

Lucca raked a hand through his hair as he stared at the door where Celina had disappeared. Had he misjudged her? Were his instincts all wrong?

Or was he just losing his touch?

The move he'd made hadn't been the smoothest he'd ever tried; he'd be the first to admit that. Something about her got under his skin He acted from instinct instead of any plan. He forgot what he was supposed to be doing, going only for what he wanted.

He hadn't intended to kiss her, at least not when he stepped into the library. The need to touch her, hold her, taste her was a sudden hunger impossible to resist. Now that he had the sweetness of her on his tongue, he only craved more.

What he wanted was Celina Steadman. It was as simple as that.

He thought she wanted him, too; he could see it in her

eyes and how she responded when he came closer than she expected. It had been clear even from a distance this morning as she stood on her balcony.

What a vision she'd been, rumpled, disheveled, sleepily sensual in her thin robe, as if she had just tumbled from her bed and, with luck, might be enticed back into it. Her flush as she met his eyes, her parted lips and the way she grasped at her open neckline had been unconscious lures. The urge to go to her, leaping from balcony to balcony, had been so strong for a moment he'd almost given in to it.

That was until she'd suddenly turned and left him there.

Something was holding her back, something to do with his grandfather.

He needed to know what it was for Nonno's sake, but also for his own. The mystery of it was driving him mad. He could think of little else, had returned this morning after only an hour at work because of it.

Well, he'd also felt a strong need to check up on her, to see what she was doing or even if she was still here. That was incidental, had nothing to do with his main purpose.

Celina had declared outright that she had no designs on Massimo. She might even be telling the truth. But if so, what did that leave?

A free vacation?

Maybe, but it seemed unlikely.

What then?

There were millions of euros in artwork housed in the palazzo.

Suppose she was checking out the place for a ring of art

thieves? It happened. The Palladino collection would be a great temptation, particularly if someone had discovered how vulnerable it was to theft.

The hair on the back of Lucca's neck tingled at the thought. He should see to it matters were better arranged. He'd have to be careful how he went about it for the sake of his grandfather's pride, but the vulnerability must come to an end.

To lose the art would be a terrible blow for Massimo, but that was not the worst of it. Learning that he had been taken in by a captivating smile and lovely form could be fatal.

It was time someone looked into the background of the lovely Signorina Celina Steadman, Lucca thought with grim conviction. Meanwhile, he would see to it she was seldom out of his sight.

Chapter Five

In the days that followed, Celina avoided Lucca as much as possible. She didn't need him constantly looking over her shoulder, for one thing, but he was also too distracting. She spent far more time than she should thinking about things he'd said or done, wondering what he thought of her, wishing he were not so mistrustful. The last thing she needed was reason for more of the same.

His kiss there in the library haunted her. She woke in the night reliving it, the tingling magic of being held close against him, his gentle expertise, also how close she'd come to being overwhelmed. Sometimes she caught herself standing on the sturdy new ladder Sergio had bought for her, pen and notebook forgotten in her hand, remembering as she stared into space.

No, she didn't need a repeat performance.

She usually rose later than she liked, waiting until she

heard the powerboat leave as Giovanni ran Lucca to his office. Only then did she venture down to breakfast. She worked quickly during his absence, cataloging and appraising works in the more public rooms. When she knew he had returned to his restoration on the palazzo and the walkway beyond its outer wall, so would be in and out at odd moments, she retreated to the back bedrooms in search of more obscure artistic works.

His project was progressing, or so it seemed. A barge laden with machinery appeared one morning and tied up at the landing area, and had been there ever since. On board was a crew dressed in heavy yellow coveralls. What they were doing was something of a mystery, but involved a monster generator that kept up a dull roar, plus what appeared to be some form of pile driver.

Lucca supervised the operation, and could often be heard shouting orders above the noise. If she sometimes paused near the salon window, smiling a little as she located his lithe form, watching the easy way he balanced on the shifting barge and his broad, emphatic gestures with both hands, that was her secret.

On days when he was detained in the heart of the city, she enjoyed relaxed and casual lunches with Massimo. When Sergio expected him home for the meal, she slipped out of the mansion to play tourist. Once, she ferried out to Murano to watch the glassblowers at work and buy glass jewelry of stunning beauty. Another time, she went to Burano for its famous lace. But her favorite escape was the winding streets and hidden campos, the building-enclosed piazzas, of Venice.

She had no set plan when she set out, seldom bothered with a map. It was amazing to be able to stroll at will where no cars or trucks were allowed, to eat at out-of-the-way restaurants, to wander in and out of the shops where nearly everything from cosmetics to clothing was faintly exotic.

She didn't mind the cold rain that often fell, even enjoyed its light tapping on her umbrella while she was buttoned up in her all-weather coat. Few were abroad then, so it almost seemed she had Venice to herself. If she lost her way, she retraced her steps until something looked familiar, or else listened for water traffic on the Grand Canal and made her way toward it. Once on the *fondamenta* that ran alongside, she walked to a vaporetto stop that would take her back to the palazzo. If all else failed, she had an app on her cell phone to guide her.

She was startled once or twice by having her bottom pinched while threading her way through crowds outside a pizzeria or bar, but wasn't bothered otherwise. She stayed alert and walked with her shoulder bag tucked against her body, but felt completely safe.

That was until the sixth or seventh time she ventured out into the city on her own.

It happened during the closing time after noon. Most shops were shut up tight behind their rolling metal shutters, and the pedestrian ways were quiet. She'd bought a bag of nougat with almonds, and was strolling along, munching the filling candy.

It was only as she entered a campo that seemed quieter,

more residential than usual, that she noticed footsteps behind her. That they were keeping pace was clear, even above the whisper of light rain falling on her umbrella.

The area was deserted and silent. The few windows that overlooked it were closed and shuttered. Sounds echoed off the surrounding stone and stucco. A chill wind shivered the surface of rainwater standing here and there in the paving.

Celina shoved her bag of candy into her coat pocket and increased her pace. She crossed the square toward an exit street that she hoped would lead toward the Grand Canal. With any luck, whoever was behind her would continue on in a different direction.

The footsteps followed.

Celina swung her umbrella aside to look over her shoulder. She could just make out the dark shape of a man wearing a soft cap pulled low over his face and with his shoulders hunched against the rain. It was possible he had business in the same direction, but what were the chances?

She faced forward again.

The street she was on narrowed up ahead, twisting away from the sounds of the canal. More of an alley than a pedestrian way, it appeared almost featureless, nothing but gray-brown walls inset with a few big, brass-studded doors.

Her sense of direction had apparently deserted her. She stared around for something, anything familiar.

There was nothing. Unease throbbed in Celina's chest with every hard beat of her heart. Reaching into her pocket, she closed her fingers around her cell and drew it out.

She bit the inside of her lip as she thought of punching

in the number for the palazzo. She had only the vaguest idea of how to tell Massimo or Sergio where she was, and no hope they could reach her before whoever was back there caught up with her. She could try Italy's version of 911, but was unsure she could she command enough Italian to explain her dilemma. And what would the police do if she were panicking for nothing, and the man on her heels was some workman late for his hot midday meal on this miserably damp day? She thumbed her phone screen to bring up the GPS app.

A shiver ran down her spine, but she shook it off. It was because of the puddle she'd just stepped in, she was sure; the water was soaking into her shoe. It had nothing to do with the harder slap of the following steps.

The phone screen blinked then bloomed into a colored map. It wasn't easy to see in the dim light, but she thought a couple of turns would take her to a bridge. Once over it, she should have a straight shot to the Grand Canal.

She set off again, quickening her steps, running a few paces then walking again. The first turn she needed was coming up. She could see it ahead of her. Just a few feet more, and she'd be on it.

A shout rang out behind her. Hard upon it was a grunted curse followed by the thud of blows. Celina whipped around. Her eyes widened at the sight of two men caught in a panting, shoving scuffle.

Abruptly, one of them tore free and dove away. He stumbled forward, half-falling, catching himself with one hand on the wet pavement. Pushing upright again, he took off down the street.

The other man pounded after him for a few steps. Then he stopped, shifted his shoulders to settle his raincoat. Shoving a hand through his hair, he turned.

Lucca.

She had known the minute she saw him. It just seemed too impossible to believe until she saw his face.

"Are you all right?" she asked, her voice a soft rasp in her throat.

He touched a knuckle to the corner of his mouth, glanced at it with a hooded gaze. "Fine."

At least he wasn't bleeding that she could see. She let out a breath she hadn't realized she was holding. "I can't believe—how on earth did you get here?"

"How do you think?" He came toward her, caught her arm and swung her into step beside him. "What in the name of heaven are you doing in this part of the city?"

"I was just walking, not going anywhere." She halted, dragging her arm free of his grasp. "You were following me. You must have been."

"What of it?"

"But why? I thought you were lunching back at—" She broke off, but not soon enough.

"Did you, now? Is that why you aren't at the palazzo? It's better to risk your pocketbook and your pretty neck than to sit down to eat with me?"

It was a figure of speech, she thought; he didn't really think she had a pretty neck. There was no cause whatever to feel flattered, or to wonder if he noticed she wasn't at lunch because he missed her.

"I'm an employee, not a guest. I'm not expected to attend every meal."

"Besides, you must get full value from your trip to Venice, yes?" He raised his hands and let them fall in a gesture of exasperation.

"I have these few hours off every day because I'm not used to a long rest after lunch."

"I doubt Nonno told you to wander around all over the city like a tourist with 'Come and get me!' tattooed on your forehead."

Her eyes narrowed. "It's better than being in the way all the time. Besides, I think you'd prefer it to having me move in on your grandfather!"

He watched her, his eyes black behind the screens of his lashes and his lips tightly folded together. The rain was increasing, beading on his hair so it curled, joining the droplets that dampened the shoulders of his overcoat. "Is that why you're rambling around like a lost soul, because of what I said?"

"I wasn't lost." She turned her attention to her umbrella as she raised it higher to protect them both.

"That isn't how it looked to me."

"Not that I don't appreciate your coming to the rescue," she went on with scrupulous honesty. "I do, I did. What I mean to say is—"

"Forget it. I'm glad I happened to be on hand."

"I wouldn't call it that, exactly." She gave him a direct look. "Who told you to follow me?"

"You are a guest in my grandfather's home. He would be devastated if anything happened to you."

"So he sent you."

"Not exactly." He reached to touch her cheek, brushing back a stray tendril of hair. "Look, we can't stand here arguing in the rain. You are pale and shaking and in strong need of a drink. I suggest we find one."

He was right, her hands were shaking. She also felt chilled to the bone, the aftermath of her moments of fear. To admit it went against the grain, however.

"Oh, I don't think—"

"I do," he said firmly. Taking her hand, he tucked it into the crook of his arm and began to walk again.

Celina didn't protest. She was more unsteady on her feet than she'd realized, for one thing. He also made her feel protected, safe, though his touch did nothing to slow her heartbeat. Until that moment, she had not realized how alone she had felt, how alone she'd been in the past few days. It was a revelation.

Lucca led them with unswerving accuracy to a small café on the Grand Canal. It was warm and steamy inside, the air rife with smells of fresh coffee, cocoa, pastries, cigarette smoke and damp wool. Though small, it seemed to be favored by the *carabinieri*, or police who kept the city safe while sporting designer uniforms. At least they were well represented at the tables.

Most of the patrons were men, Celina noticed as she cradled her espresso strengthened by grappa between the palms of her hand, at least at this time of day. That was probably why she drew so many stares. After what had happened earlier, it made her vaguely uncomfortable.

"You're all right now? You're sure?" Lucca asked.

"Totally." His concern was genuine, she thought, even if he didn't like or trust her.

He pushed the cream-filled coronet he'd ordered toward her. "Eat this, and I'll get another."

"I couldn't. Really."

"Because you don't want it or because it's necessary to disagree with everything I say?"

He sounded so aggrieved she couldn't help smiling a little. "I had candy for lunch. I don't think adding a pastry to it is going to help."

"*Per l'amor de Dio.* Why did you not say?" Leaving his chair in a swift, lithe move, he went to place another order at the counter.

~ ~ ~

Lucca leaned back in his chair, brushing flakey crumbs of coronet dough from his coat while watching Celina eat a slice of pizza thick with vegetables, sausage and cheese. Color was beginning to come back into her cheeks. He was profoundly grateful for it.

He had left it nearly too late back there in the alley. Some moronic part of him had thought she should have a small fright to teach her greater caution in her exploration of the city. Well, and because she dared prefer her own company to his, so had frustrated his grand scheme for days. He was not proud of the impulse, particularly when she expressed her gratitude. He could have caught up with her earlier and saved her the nervous moments.

Of course, she might not have been nearly as glad to see him.

He'd expected her to spot him trailing after her long before. It had been especially difficult to remain out of sight on the ferry to Murano. The urge to fake a meeting, to pretend surprise at seeing her, had been near irresistible. He'd longed to show her all the marvels she'd seen on her own, to buy for her every glass bauble she smiled over in the shops.

The results of his investigation might have some bearing on that generous impulse. Celina Steadman did not appear in any criminal database anywhere. Her background was exactly as she claimed. She was the daughter of middle-class parents from the northeastern United States, father deceased, mother long employed as a buyer for a department chain. She was also the granddaughter of a well-known painter of New England seascapes and shorelines. She had graduated from university with an art degree, was the designated art expert at an auction house who had, almost by accident, become an authority on Canaletto.

He had misjudged her, perhaps, and yet something was still not right.

Nonetheless, he now knew her far better than he had before. He'd watched her taste his city as a person of discernment tasted fine wine, talking easily with the shop-keeper who fashioned carnival masks in his back workroom, caressing fine pottery, closing her eyes to inhale the fragrance of soaps made of goat's milk and herbs and flowers. He'd seen her absorbing the life on the canals, standing in the very center of their bridges and looking both forward and back, had waited while she drifted through museums with intense interest in her eyes and no small understanding of what she was seeing.

She even seemed to like the endless rain, which came very close to making her an honorary Venetian.

Observing her every movement, Lucca had felt an almost painful need to take her hand, to pull her close against him and turn her face up to his. He'd wanted to taste the salt on her lips after she's braved the chill sea wind, to hold her against the heat of his body when she was cold, to sit with her while she watched the sunset glaze the sea with shades of red and gold, and see the same colors come and go in her eyes. And more. Much more.

Moronic indeed.

She was in his thoughts far too often for comfort. He recognized the danger, knew well it would not do to become too intrigued. That was a pitfall he must and would resist. Whatever she was about in Venice, she would not stay. Like her grandmother before her, she would take what she wanted from the city and then return to her life in the States.

Not that he desired anything else. No, far from it.

Still, she hadn't deserved to learn fear of his Venice, this grand old Queen of the Adriatic. It was far less dangerous than many places in the world.

He had been afraid enough for both of them for a

moment or two, there earlier. The surge of adrenaline that pumped in its wake had made him less than kind, as well as indiscreet.

It was a mistake he would remedy as best he could. Also one he would not make again.

Chapter Six

It was a couple of days later that Celina returned to her room after lunch and found large pale gray boxes stacked on her bed. She'd not noticed when they were delivered, but then she'd been busy all morning in the long gallery at the rear of the palazzo.

She stared at them a moment before her face cleared. The name of the shop emblazoned on them in gold lettering gave away their contents. It was *La Mascherata,* The Masquerade.

This must be the costume for *carnevale* Massimo had promised.

She thought he'd forgotten, as nothing more had been said since it was first mentioned. It wasn't as if there'd been no opportunity. Since the stalker incident, she had seldom been out of his sight. He sought her out at odd moments, checking to see which canvas was her focus, telling her whatever he knew about how it had come into the family, or helping to move her ladder from one place to the next.

When Massimo was not there, it was Lucca who hunted her down. He was concentrating on shoring up the canal wall outside the palazzo almost full time now, or so it seemed. She never knew when she would look down and see him standing below her. Almost against her will, she began to listen for his footsteps, to glance around at every small sound in case he appeared.

He was charming, always interested in what she was doing, and often the bearer of an espresso, pastry or impromptu lunch that they spread on a handy table or the floor. He made her laugh with tales of his boyhood spent rattling around in the huge old house, hiding from Massimo, his grandmother and Sergio for the fun of it, or else seeing how loud everyone would shout when he walked the loggia railing as if balancing on a tightrope.

She was touched by his stoicism as he spoke of how his father had died in a boating accident when he was nine. Also of the day his mother left him with Massimo while she went on her honeymoon after remarrying, but never came back for him, moving to Rome instead with her new husband.

When Celina did leave the palazzo, Lucca acted as her escort. She allowed it, not out of fear but for Massimo's peace of mind.

Rambling here and there with him was amazing fun as he kept up a barrage of wry and pointed comments while taking her places she'd never have found on her own. She grew to expect the feel of his guiding hand at her back, his strong arm bracing her against him as they rode a bucking vaporetto, his smiling deference and meticulous manners. She came to anticipate the small gifts he bought and presented as if they were such nothings it would be silly to refuse them.

Then there was his game of dropping brief kisses on her lips every time they crossed a bridge. And Venice was overrun with bridges.

Celina was bemused, yet frustrated. Was Lucca serious or only being attentive at Massimo's request? Did he feel something for her or was he playing some odd game? Either way, she didn't need the distraction of his presence or the hum of unsatisfied longing being with him aroused inside her.

She had to get on with the search that had brought her. The days were flying past, and she'd found nothing. She could stretch her time here only so far, and then she'd have to go.

She thought about it often, but thinking didn't get the job done.

With a quick shake of her head, Celina reached for the largest of the three boxes on the bed. She untied the ribbon that fastened it and lifted away the lid. Then she stood for several seconds with the breath caught in her throat. Gently, then, she laid the lid aside.

Her sigh was soft with amazement and her hands not quite steady as she lifted the dress of the costume from the nest of tissue paper. It was rich aqua blue in color, a marvelous confection of satin, lace and silk illusion with a full skirt that was draped and tucked and swathed within an inch of its life. Gloriously elaborate, it had an eighteenth century look to it, but was actually of no particular era. Set within the pattern of the lace on the boned bodice were literally thousands of small iridescent beads, considerably more expensive versions of the beads she sometimes braided into her hair. A petticoat was included which would make for a froth of skirts.

The second box held a full-face mask of silver-painted papier-mâché. Beside it was a curled wig dyed a shining aqua and topped by a small, heart-shaped hat in the same colors as the dress and just as gloriously draped. The contents of the third box completed the ensemble with a matching velvet cloak, stockings and silk slippers with kitten heels.

This was no costume off the rack, Celina thought as she lifted a layer of the silk illusion and let it fall, watching its rainbow-like shimmer that held hints of silver, rose and lavender along with aqua. It was a couturier's fantasy designed specifically for carnival romance. A dream costume, it was as lovely and impractical as any conjured up by a fairy godmother. The woman who wore it would feel like Cinderella setting out on a night of enchantment.

With abrupt decision, Celina tucked the various pieces of the ensemble back into their boxes and closed the lids. If the whole thing had been less glamorous, less high couture, it might have been all right. This one must have cost a fortune. She couldn't possibly accept anything so out of her league. She just couldn't.

"Why must you refuse this costume?" Massimo asked in pained tones when she ran him to earth where he sat dozing in his favorite chair in the salon. "Do you not like it?"

"Of course I like it, it's beyond beautiful. But that's the problem. It's just too much."

"Nonsense! You will carry it off to perfection. Nothing could ever be too much for you."

His certainty made her feel warm inside, but she still shook her head. "I don't think so. I'm not used to designer clothing."

"But what's to be done with it if you won't have it?"

"Send it back. I'm sure selling it to someone else will be no problem."

A stern look settled over his lined features. "This I cannot do."

"Of course you can. People return things all the time."

"Not from this house. Besides, Lucca will look ridiculous without you to set off his costume in the same style."

She tried to picture Lucca in aqua silk, but failed. "You can't be serious."

"But yes, I assure you. It is all the rage just now, these matching costumes for men and women. Besides, he will think you don't approve of his choice."

"His choice?"

"But of course." Massimo spread his hands. "What do I know of such things? I, who have not ventured out onto the canals for *carnevale* in years? Lucca offered to select this costume for you and I was happy to leave it to him."

"I know it should go back, then!"

"So you would deliberately embarrass him with your rejection of his choice?"

"Not deliberately, no, but—"

"So I thought. You could not be so unkind. Besides, you must wear something to the Toso ball."

He had a point. Celina bit the inside of her bottom lip as she considered it. She'd tried to forget the ball since she wasn't sure she'd attend. She'd never been to such a fancy affair. No matter what Massimo said, she couldn't think she'd fit in, could easily picture herself skulking around the edges or hiding out behind a column or potted plant.

What was with this fancy costume anyway? Was it another way for Lucca to provide for her entertainment? Or could it simply be how things were done in Venice among the elite? Was she showing her total lack of sophistication by protesting?

"Please, *cara*, this matter of a costume is a mere nothing. Wear it to make an old man happy?"

If he put it that way, how could she refuse?

Yet a niggling suspicion remained, eating away at her confidence right up until the time came to dress for the family dinner that would precede the dratted ball.

Celina showered away the ancient dust and fibers she'd acquired during the day from the disintegrating wood of old picture frames. She blow-dried her hair, but twisted it into a loose knot on top of her head since she would be wearing the wig. Makeup might also have been unnecessary, given the mask, except she would naturally not be wearing it during dinner. She took her time with the cosmetics, then, applying peach gloss, highlighting her cheekbones and adding smoky liner and subtle aqua shadows to her eyelids for a bit of drama.

She thought getting into the dress of the costume would require help from one of the maids, but finally managed it on her own. The wig with its small, provocative hat was only slightly less of a problem. With it firmly in place, she stepped into the silk heels and turned to look at herself in the long mirrored door of the *armadio*, the wardrobe that served as a closet.

She hardly recognized herself. She seemed an exotic yet ethereal stranger, almost as if she belonged in the Venetian bedroom behind her. It was gratifying and yet disturbing, as if she were pretending to be something she wasn't.

She picked up the silver mask, held it up before her face and turned to the mirror again. It had the impassive beauty of regular, even features. Regardless, something about it made her eyes, seen through its holes, appear brilliant with excitement, while the half-parted lips suggested breathless anticipation. The combined expression was disturbing in a way she could not quite grasp.

Who could have guessed a costume would make such a difference?

At least she wouldn't be an embarrassment to Massimo during this evening with his family, she thought. She was a little nervous of meeting them all, his sister and her son, plus several cousins near his age with their wives and grown children.

Of course, it hardly mattered what they thought of her as she would soon be gone from their lives. Spinning away from her reflection, she left the room and made her way down to the salon.

Celina half feared she might be the only person in such an extravagant costume during Massimo's dinner before the ball. She need not have worried. Pausing in the doorway, she saw the salon was awash in silk and satin, lace and velvet. Every color of the rainbow was represented, most appearing in ensembles far more ostentatious than her own.

Tightness she had not recognized until that moment eased from her chest. She was able to smile as she walked into the room.

"*Cara*! How fine you look." Massimo, dressed in navy blue embroidered with gold, like some courtier of a vanished century, called out that compliment as he strode toward her with arms outstretched. Catching her hands, he held them wide for his appraisal. "*Molto, molto bella*! There are no words to describe how lovely, though I knew it must be this way. Come now, allow me to introduce you to everyone."

She looked at once for Lucca, though only as a familiar face among the strangers. That was all, of course. He stood at the far end of the room, talking with a young couple dressed in matching purple and with similar beehive headdresses on their heads. Drink in hand, he turned slowly as if he sensed she was there.

He appeared as elegant as his ancestor on the wall behind him, and every bit as devastating. The costume he wore was a match for hers in color and fabric, just as Massimo had promised, but there the resemblance ended. Where hers appeared utterly feminine, his silk and satin made such a stark contrast against his olive skin and strong features that it highlighted his virility.

His gaze was dark between eyelids narrowed with assessment as he surveyed her slowly from head to toe. Then a slow smile lifted a corner of his mouth, rising to warm his eyes with the wicked, golden gleams so devastating to her equilibrium. He lifted the glass he held in silent salute.

It was the most gallant compliment she'd ever received in her life. It warmed her to the center of her being, while every inch of her body tingled as at a physical touch. She felt truly beautiful as she put her hand through the arm Massimo offered and let him lead her into the crowd.

Dinner was half over before the glow of the evening dulled for her. The cause was a simple question from Massimo's sister, Sofia, who sat next to her. The lady was of undetermined age but well-preserved appearance, round-faced and pleasant in a costume of forest green silk with French influence and a high-piled powdered wig of the Sun King's court. Until that moment, her conversation had been about her physical ailments, fear of the flu that was spreading in the city, her dogs and her grandchildren.

"How charming you look in your costume, Signorina Steadman. You and Lucca are most beautifully matched. How is it the two of you have become close when we have not met before?"

"Oh, we aren't that close." The reply was offhand, for Celina's attention was on something Lucca, sitting directly across from her, was saying to a sloe-eyed, dark-haired lady on his right. She was a cousin, if Celina remembered correctly, though she didn't act much like it. On the woman's other side was Ernesto, Sofia's stolid and overweight younger son of about forty who was paying more attention to his dinner than the conversation going on around him.

Massimo's sister raised an artfully drawn brow. "Yet you wear the costumes of an engaged pair or those newly married? Come, now. Do I detect a whirlwind romance? Or has he merely been keeping you to himself?"

Celina felt the heat of a flush rising to her hairline as she gave Sofia her complete attention. "An engaged couple?"

"But of course? Who else would wish to be so similar?"

"I didn't realize."

"Of course, she didn't, *Zia* Sofia, and naturally she isn't," Lucca said, entering their conversation with an amused air. "You must not confuse our guest. I only ordered matching costumes as an aid in keeping track of Celina at the ball."

"I'm sure, *caro mio*," his great-aunt said with a dry note in her voice. "Whatever you say."

It was clear Sofia suspected something more to the situation, but at least she didn't pursue it. Celina was relieved, though something in Lucca's dark gaze as it held hers made her pulse flutter in her veins.

Were matching costumes for carnival really the next thing to a promise of a future together? Surely not, and yet she couldn't help wondering how many others in the room looked at them that way. Much of her earlier pleasure in the ensemble faded, replaced by discomfort. She almost felt as if Lucca had claimed her in some odd fashion.

She had no time to dwell on it, however. Sofia, taking a bite of bread then chasing it with a swallow of wine, spoke again.

"I must say you look familiar to me, Celina," she said, her eyes narrowing a little as she considered her. "You are amazingly like someone I knew many years ago."

"Am I?"

"She was also American," Sofia went on in her carrying, high-pitched tones. "I remember her hair above all. It was so pale in color, so long and shining. She was glamorous beyond belief to a mere adolescent who had never known anyone from the States before."

Celina lifted her chin as her every sense went on alert. "Oh?"

"I thought she must be a movie star. She was so free in her manner, you know, and in the way she walked and talked. My mother did not at all approve, but I longed to be just like her."

"What was her name? Do you recall?"

"Mary, I think—No, that's not right. It was something a bit more ... Marilee! That was it."

Celina could feel her heart begin to race at that familiar name. "Where was it that you met?"

"Why, here and there, in restaurants and cafes, even once here at the palazzo. She was always with Massimo that summer. My mother greatly feared he would marry her, but it came to nothing."

Lucca was still watching them, Celina knew. A frown drew his brows together and his fingers where he gripped his fork were white at the tips. She tried for a light tone as she answered the woman at her side. "Just a fling, I suppose."

"So one would think, but the family was concerned for some time. I remember that well. Massimo was not himself after she went away."

"But he recovered." Celina glanced down the table to where her host sat at its head, talking quietly to an elderly relative. If he heard any part of what they were saying, he gave no sign.

"True." Sofia gave a shake of her head that threatened to dislodge her wig. "He married a short time later, though it was not a happy alliance. Some say it was this Marilee's fault." She glanced quickly at Lucca across the table, and then gave a dismissive shrug. "But tell me, *cara*. What think you of this *Pollo all Merengo*? Is it not perfection?"

Celina could not be sure if her dinner companion was really that enthused over the chicken with tomatoes and olives or had been reminded of discretion by her nephew's scowl. Either way, she expected to hear more about that gossipy exchange before the evening was over.

The moment came as soon as she entered the salon after dinner. Lucca caught up with her inside the doorway. Placing a hand at her back, he directed her toward a corner sofa at the furthest distance from the fire.

Celina went with him willingly enough. It seemed the time for avoiding the facts was past.

"Who is Marilee? Yes, and what is she to you?"

He threw the questions at her almost before they were seated. She might have known he would come straight to the point.

"She was my grandmother," she said evenly. "You heard about her the first day we met."

His gaze upon her face was steady, watchful. "The one whose house you inherited?"

She nodded, more pleased than she wanted to be that he'd remembered. "The artist who came to Venice to study."

"For the summer."

"As it happened, though I suppose it might have been any time of year."

Lucca glanced around, but there was no one near enough to overhear what they were saying. "She and Nonno were—involved."

"For a short while, until she returned home."

"It meant nothing to her, this affair of theirs. She went away and left him without a backward glance." His voice was rough as he made that accusation. Celina couldn't let it pass, though she had some idea of how he felt. "I wouldn't say that. It was just that she had obligations and duties back home. She'd just graduated from college, and the trip to Italy was a gift from her parents. She was also involved with someone she'd known most of her life but who was in the military. It was understood the time in Venice was a month or two of freedom before going back home and getting on with real life."

"So that's what she did."

Celina tipped her head in assent. "You could say that. She did what was expected of her like a good girl from the Sixties. She married the soldier who was her fiancé, and who was home on leave by the time she got back, possibly because he suspected she was becoming too involved in Venice. They soon had two children and a house in the suburbs."

"Not to mention a country cottage where she went to paint."

"That's right, though she bought that for herself after she began to sell her work."

"And they lived happily ever after, I suppose."

Her smile was brief. "Not exactly."

"Don't tell me she regretted leaving Italy."

"All right, I won't tell you," she returned at once, stung by the skepticism in his voice.

Grandma Marilee certainly had her regrets, though she'd never paraded them for all to see. She'd always declared that people didn't take enough chances, that they let life pass them by while things just happened to them or other people made decisions for them. Her favorite movie had been *Auntie Mame*, with its famous quote, 'Live! Life is a banquet, and most poor suckers are starving to death.'

"So she told you of her time here with Nonno."

"She spoke of Venice often, but that's all. I only read about their relationship recently, in the journal she kept during her time here."

It had been more of a notebook, that particular volume, one filled with dozens of Venetian sketches alongside the written text. Studies of Massimo had been included as well, detailed drawings of his face in different moods, of his hands, his ears, his eyes. There'd also been a single drawing of his upper body, half nude, unfinished, but Lucca didn't need to know that.

He stared at her for a long moment while the groove between his brows deepened. "Having read about the two of them, you decided—what? What made you come?"

"Curiosity, I suppose."

"Curiosity."

"What else?" It was an effort to keep her voice level, but she managed it. She'd also come for the mystery of what might have been, but wasn't sure Lucca was ready to hear that part.

"I don't know what else," he said slowly, "though I'm beginning to think it was something less than a coincidence that Nonno heard about you and the painting you found."

She resented the implication too much to answer it, even indirectly, though it held a grain of truth. Her boss at the auction house had discovered Massimo's contact information and forwarded the article about her, though it had been at her suggestion.

"The question in my mind is why," Lucca went on. "Why were you so determined to get to my grandfather?"

"I thought you had that all figured out," she answered on a short laugh.

"If I thought—" he began.

"*Dio*, there you are," Massimo exclaimed as he came toward them, carrying his mask and cloak and with Sergio following with those for Celina and Lucca. "Are the two of you quarreling again? I could almost believe you do it for the joy of making up."

"Oh, no—" Celina began.

"Yes, of course. Why else?" Lucca's deeper voice overrode her lighter tones. His smile even appeared genuine as he got to his feet and took Celina's hand, pulling her up beside him.

"You have my permission to quarrel as often as you please then," his grandfather said, his voice as warm as the twinkle in his eyes. "But come now, we depart. It's time to go to the ball."

~ ~ ~

"Who is she?"

The question came from Patrizio, Lucca's friend from university days who stood with him and three or four others near the bandstand. It was a protective cluster, though none were willing to admit it. Something about the masked anonymity of a ball during *carnevale* seemed to bring out the huntress in women. No matter how diligent a man was about keeping his costume secret, they always discovered it. Large sums had been known to change hands for the sake of such information.

The woman Patrizio watched as he spoke had no need of such tactics. A vision in aqua silk and wafting draperies, she seemed not to know there was a man in the room other than the one who led her in a lilting waltz. Though her mask was without expression, her eyes shone through its slits, laughing up at Massimo as he swung her with expertise gained from years of ballroom dancing.

Massimo wore no mask to hide his lined features. He gazed down at his partner with affection so open it was almost painful to see it.

"My grandfather's house guest," Lucca answered in clipped tones.

"Lucky Nonno."

"Not that kind of guest."

"*Mi dispiace.* Sorry." Patrizio hesitated. "But are you sure?"

"Considering my grandfather, yes."

"Then why is it he who is dancing with the beautiful one, instead of you?"

It was a good question.

For the past two hours, Celina had whirled around the floor with others while Lucca stood and watched. Her enjoyment of the evening was contagious, so free and natural compared to the blasé boredom of others. Partners were drawn to her like kids to gelato. And so was he, if it came to that.

He'd started toward her a dozen times, only to change his mind. She might refuse his request after their earlier confrontation, and then where would he be?

"Look out. Here comes trouble," Patrizio muttered.

It was Zia Sofia bearing down upon them. She bustled into their midst like a plump goose among pigeons, scattering his friends just as easily. Lucca was tempted to make his escape, too, except he knew she would come after him.

"You must do something, Lucca," his aunt said, catching his arm and pulling him close while she shrilled in his ear. "That's unless you want a grandmother younger than you are. Have you no concept of the danger?"

"Nonno is old enough to know what he's doing." His shrug was offhand. It was one thing to form daring schemes himself, but something else for them to be demanded of him.

"Don't be naive, my dear nephew. Massimo is a lamb to the slaughter, and a willing one at that."

"But are you certain Celina has a knife?" Watching her, following her tender curves with his gaze, it was almost impossible to believe she was anything other than exactly what she claimed.

"What?" Zia Sofia stared at him without comprehension.

"Nothing." He went on after a second. "I thought the two of you hit it off at dinner."

"Oh, she is likeable enough, I'll grant you that much. And it was all right as long as I thought the two of you were together, one way or another."

"Now you don't?"

"Not while you stand here with your hands in your pockets while Massimo makes a fool of himself. Have you no better sense than to let it happen? Do you want her as a member of the family?"

He stiffened. "She said something to make you think

that's her aim?"

"When have I had time to speak with her again with Massimo monopolizing her every moment? Yet what else could it mean when a young woman prefers to dance with a man so much older? Yes, and especially while the most handsome man in Venice stands by doing nothing?"

"Don't tell me she refused to dance with Ernesto?" As he spoke, a possible explanation struck him full force. But no, it was too unlikely. For one thing, Nonno was not, and never had been, so lacking in honor or concern for those close to him. Then the timing was all wrong, he was almost sure of it.

"I mean you, of course, Lucca, though my Ernesto waits for his chance. Only look at him, hanging around like a lapdog begging for pasta."

She was right. The waltz playing these past few minutes was winding down. Ernesto was shuffling, shifting his bulk as if ready to make his move the instant it stopped.

The thought of Celina in his cousin's arms, held against his pudgy body by sweaty hands, made the top of Lucca's head feel hot. He looked from her to Ernesto and back again.

"Excuse me," he said to Zia Sofia without taking his eyes off Celina again. "I believe it's time I made a move."

Celina and Nonno had come to a halt at the edge of the dance floor, in the cool draft from open French doors that stirred the palm tree in its ceramic urn beside them. Lucca's long strides carried him past Ernesto, so he arrived first in front of his quarry. As she turned to face him, he thought he caught a flash of relief in the clear blue of her eyes. At least, he preferred to think so, even as he was amazed that it mattered to him.

"May I?" he asked, offering his hand.

Her smile was tentative before she glanced at his grandfather.

"By all means," Nonno said at once. "It will give an old man time to catch his breath."

"Oh, please," she said with the lightest of laughs, "it's you who nearly danced me off my feet."

"Go, go," Massimo said with a wave of his hand, "before I start to believe you!"

The gesture and words were fond, but no more, Lucca thought. If his grandfather was jealous at being asked to share Celina's company, he hid it well. Still, he felt as if he had carried off the prize as he led her onto the floor.

The music was another waltz, though one with a faster tempo. The choice might be uninspired, but was also unsurprising for a ball hosted by those his grandfather's age. It was just as well. Frenzied gyrating to something more modern would wreak havoc on the elaborate costumes now swirling about on the dance floor.

Celina might look wraithlike in the soft color and airy fabrics she wore, but was real enough in his arms, firm where she should be firm, soft otherwise. She danced well, was instantly responsive to his slightest movement.

It was impossible not to wonder if she would be the same in the arms of a lover.

The mere thought caused a too firm reminder of his

pledge to seduce her. Even as it shifted through his mind, he was forced to wonder if it was no more than an excuse. The feel of her against him, the elusive scent she wore that might be her shampoo, the mystery of the mask that concealed her features, fired his blood until it pooled in places that grew less comfortable by the minute. He moved with precision yet by rote, plagued by sensations as troubling as they were inescapable.

Somewhere within his unsavory purpose lay a pitfall he'd not seen before. But what were the odds? It was too late to worry about it now.

"I haven't thanked you for my costume," she said with stilted politeness.

"What?" He tilted his head, trying to see behind the mask she wore.

"It's the most gorgeous thing I've ever worn. Massimo said you chose it."

His grandfather sometimes talked too much. "It was no great effort, a matter of walking into a shop and pointing."

It had actually taken seven phone calls, visits to five different shops and most of two afternoons, but there was no need to say so. The aqua color picked up the intriguing blend of blues and greens in her eyes. He had made certain of it.

"You're positive?"

"*Certo*," he said with all the firmness he could muster. The determination that had driven him was merely in his nature. There was no other reason.

"I hope you will let me repay you."

"No."

"Why not? Don't tell me it's some Italian machismo thing."

"Forget it. It's nothing." The last thing he wanted was to get into her costume's price, or that of his own which was so faithful a match. Beyond that, he enjoyed the idea that he'd chosen what she wore against the softness of her skin. It was return enough.

"Well, it's something to me. In fact, it means a great deal."

He smiled, he couldn't help it, at that backhanded indication of how much she prized his choice. "You're more than welcome."

"I meant I dislike being so indebted."

"I know, but let it go, if you please."

"I can't do that. Your aunt said—"

"I heard what she said," he interrupted, his voice gruff, "and it's nonsense."

"So you didn't buy this costume to make it appear we are a couple."

"Would that have been so bad?"

The look in her blue eyes was like glacier ice. "Only if it was also to prevent people thinking I was with Massimo."

"So it would be okay if I set out to mark you as mine?" he asked with dry logic.

"I didn't say that!"

It was remotely possible he had meant to make a statement of some kind, but of what variety he wasn't sure. It had been an impulse, these mated costumes, one based on a vision of how he thought she might look in carnival regalia. No doubt he should have thought it through more completely, but it was too late to worry about that now.

"No, you didn't," he said, relenting with a quick shake of his head. "Look, it was just a whim, a way to help you feel a part of things and, as I said before, to keep an eye on you in this crowd. No deeper meaning is involved and no obligation, I promise you."

"I never thought there was an obligation." Her gaze was less chilly than before.

"No. Well, none except that you wear it with pleasure and in good health."

She gazed up at him for long seconds while they whirled in the dance. Lucca wanted to tear off the mask she wore to discover her exact expression, perhaps read how she felt as she stared into his eyes, what she thought of what he'd said, whether she believed it.

He also longed to know how she felt at being in his arms. It would not be wise, he knew, but that didn't make it less compelling.

After a moment, she looked away past his shoulder. He thought he heard her sigh.

It was stifling in the ballroom from the press of bodies and overworked heating. The day had been clear for a change, with pale sunshine that inched temperatures higher. Yet Lucca could feel the extra moisture in the air that foretold more rain.

Midnight was drawing near. Dinner had been late even by Italian standards, and then it had taken time to organize and make the transfer to the palazzo. The ball had been in full swing when they arrived, and would go on until dawn. Diehards would stay until the last note was played, wringing the final ounce of enjoyment from this, one of the last great balls of the *carnevale* season. But others less hardy were already beginning to make their farewells and trail away toward the exit.

"You are enjoying the ball?" he asked as he glanced down at the averted mask that was Celina's face.

"It's been a wonderful experience. I wouldn't have missed it for the world."

"But you are tiring of it, perhaps?"

She looked up. "What makes you think so?"

"Nothing in particular. It just occurred to me that you are among strangers, in spite of Nonno's best efforts." If his suggestion had other implications, that was his affair.

"There is that."

It was tacit agreement, and that was enough. "We could go, if it pleases you."

"You wouldn't mind?"

"I've had enough, in all truth, and I suspect Nonno will not object." As she stared up at him as if trying to judge the sincerity of his claim, he went on. "We need not go straight back to the palazzo. There is a full moon tonight, and it occurs to me I have yet to show you the Campo di San Marco in moonlight."

"So you haven't."

"Shall we then?"

"*Certo*," she answered.

Lucca thought she smiled behind her mask. At least he hoped so.

Chapter

Seven

S

t. Mark's Square was deserted. It stretched ghostly still under the cool light of the moon, with the domed and spired wonderments of the basilica and many-arched Doge's Palace lying to one side. On the other were deserted restaurants and other buildings, while the shifting, lapping waters of the lagoon lay just beyond where Celina and Lucca stood.

The stones of the paved area that stretched before them glistened wetly, and standing pools of water were everywhere. Wind swirled through the vast, open space, and the tower of the campanile lifted into the night sky, casting its long shadow in a sharp, black diagonal.

Nothing moved. The only artificial light came from the lamps like ornate antique lanterns that topped posts here and there. And the full glory of the moon poured down over all of it with silver benediction.

Celina breathed the humid, salt-tinged air deep into her lungs while her heart swelled with the beauty around her and magic of the moment. This was something she wouldn't have missed for anything, something else she would remember for the rest of her life.

Standing there with her hands thrust into the inside pockets of her cloak, wearing costume and mask as so many must have before her through the centuries, it was easy to imagine being a part of this old city's vibrant past, easy to realize the square must have lain in the moonlight here on this piece of soggy land exactly like this for centuries.

To picture the old Conte Lucca di Palladino striding across the square on some midnight errand, cloak swirling and plumed hat blown by the wind, was also easy. Especially as she had his near replica standing at her side.

"It's just lovely," she said, her voice not quite even. "Thank you so much for bringing me here."

"It is my pleasure and my honor."

She looked up at Lucca in his own cloak and wig, wide cavalier's hat and silver mask. He was a stranger and yet intimately familiar. Mysterious, innately sensual, he seemed dangerously close as he blocked the chill wind off the lagoon with his broad shoulders.

He meant what he said, she thought. He was a part of his city and it was part of him. She could not imagine him anywhere else. Even Massimo, with his gallant ways and occasional lapses into the Venetian dialect was not quite so steeped in the life of Venice. And that was incredibly seductive.

Lucca Palladino was, in many ways, a man with whom she could easily fall in love. She was halfway there already in this dreamlike moment.

"It's too bad Massimo didn't come with us," she said as a counter to her wayward thoughts.

"He has seen it many times."

"I suppose he must have, at that." They had let Lucca's nonno off at the palazzo on their way, and their driver, Giovanni, as well. Lucca had taken the wheel of the powerboat for the fast run to the square.

The wind whipped around them in a sudden gust. The moon dimmed as a gray-purple veil of clouds crossed its face. Water from the lagoon lapped over the lip of the gondola landing not far away. It fanned out, spreading toward them in a dark, gliding sheet.

"Oh, look." Amazement threaded Celina's voice as she watched the encroaching water.

"It is the high tide," Lucca said in explanation, "and a moon tide at that."

Celina nodded her understanding, but shivered anyway as the wetness washed around the soles of her silk shoes. They were made for dancing, not wading in water.

"Cold?" Lucca asked in low-voiced concern.

"A little," she conceded as dampness seeped into the silk over her toes and a wind gust swirled inside the opening of her cloak.

"Here, let me warm you."

Abruptly she was enveloped in the heavier folds of his cloak, also in his male heat and scents of warm silk and tantalizing male cologne. Another tremor moved over her, one that had little to do with wind and water. She stood perfectly still, as if that might quiet the sudden turmoil inside her.

She wanted to lean into Lucca, to turn and press against his hard form from her breasts to knees. The power of that need was so strong that she felt her eyes water with it. She turned her head to look up at him. Another wave topped the seawall at the landing and slid toward them, but Celina barely noticed.

He was watching her, his eyes dark within the almond-shaped holes of his mask. The silver papier-mâché of it gave no hint of what he felt or thought, yet she could not look away. They had argued earlier, but it made little difference. The heightened emotion between them was like a force field drawing them together.

Lucca shifted then, lifting an arm through the slit of his cloak. With a single move, he ripped off his mask and let it fall. Reaching for hers, he lifted it away, disentangled it from her wig and hat to hold it by its elastic band. His gaze searched her face, her eyes, there in the nighttime darkness and damp of the square. Then he lowered his head and set his mouth to hers.

This was exactly what she craved, though she had not known it until that instant. She'd longed to feel his lips, so hot and expertly savoring, upon hers, to taste him as he traced with his tongue the line where hers opened. She wanted his sweetness and moisture, the faint prickle of his beard at the corners of his mouth, the sensation of becoming one with him.

She gave a soft moan as she turned and circled his waist with her arms beneath his cloak, sliding spread hands over the firm muscles of his back. Her breasts tingled, swelling as she pressed against him, and she shivered again at gratification of her secret longing.

He drew her closer, one hand smoothing the indentation of her waist, sliding upward to rest against the curve of her breast. He deepened the kiss, invading in sure possession and the imitation of one more complete.

It was elemental, a part of the night, an ending that had been implicit in the beginning of this midnight view of the square. She recognized it now, this urge toward physical contact. It had not come from him alone; she acknowledged that as well. She had wanted to be with him, to touch him and be touched by him.

She closed her hand on the jacket of his costume, fisting the heavy silk as she clung to him. She could not get close enough. Her chest ached with pent breath and need. Her stomach muscles clenched with the drawing depths of it. She had never felt like this before, as if the dark mystery of the square, the moonlight and rising tide were a part of the man who held her.

The sudden blast of a siren shattered the night, becoming a strident wail that rose and fell with ear-numbing cadence. It came from close by, sounding as if it was almost on top of them. At the same time, a cold wave surged around Celina's ankles, one so strong it threatened to undermine her footing. She gasped as if suddenly waking.

Don't worry," Lucca said against the corner of her mouth. "It's only the warning for *acqua alta*, the high water."

"But my shoes, this expensive costume—"

"Neither matters as long as you are all right. For that, I have you. You're safe with me."

He bent then to sweep her up against his chest. She gave a small yelp in the moment before he caught her closer. Then he was moving with swift, splashing steps, heading toward the lagoon as if he meant to walk into its rising night-black waters.

He didn't, of course. It was only her disoriented fantasy that made her think he might. That and the way the powerboat in which they had arrived floated even with the gondola landing now, riding high on the tide.

Lucca reached it and bundled her aboard. Celina ducked inside the cabin, grateful to be out of the chill and damp wind.

She was also glad to be out of Lucca's arms, or so she told herself as she watched him release the boat's mooring line then leap aboard. The more space she put between them, the better. She could not think while he held her close, and she needed to do that, needed it desperately.

The trip home was rough. The water was choppy, blown into whitecap-topped waves by the wind. They bounced and wallowed with the roar of the motor rising and falling as if it might quit at any moment. The night grew blacker and rain began to fall, beating the water ahead of them into froth, dashing against the windscreen so it was difficult to see more than a few feet in front of them.

Lucca steered through it all with calm assurance, as if it was nothing out of the ordinary. He seemed to keep his heading through the main canal by sheer instinct.

Celina sat beside him, holding on with clenched teeth, chilled from the wind, her wet feet and the loss of his arms around her. Yet she couldn't stop watching him in the lights from the dashboard, thinking of his ancestors who had made these waters their playground for centuries, strong, fearless, effortlessly charismatic men too handsome for their own good.

At last the palazzo came into view. Bringing the powerboat alongside the landing was no easy feat, though Sergio and Giovanni hurried out to secure it. Celina was helped from it first. She stood for an instant under the protection of an umbrella put up by Sergio, watching as Lucca leaped out, trading places with Giovanni who would put the sleek craft away.

What would she and Lucca do once they were inside? Would he expect to take up where they'd left off when interrupted by the siren?

Panic gripped her at the thought. She hesitated a moment, but then backed away. Calling a hasty goodnight toward where he was still holding the rocking powerboat, she turned and ran for the safety of her room.

Once inside, she kicked off her wet shoes, fought her way out of her costume. Running a hot bath, she sank into it. Though she lay in the water for some time, she still could not get warm. Climbing out, she skimmed through her nighttime ritual, pulled on pajamas and ran for the bed.

She lay huddled under the covers, listening to the rain falling on the balcony outside the French doors, replaying the moments in Lucca's arms over and over again.

She had not known she could feel like that. Nothing had prepared her for it. None of the brief boy-girl romances of her teens or college days had included anything remotely like the emotional onslaught she'd passed through there in the square.

How ironic that she should experience that awakening now, with this man. It really wasn't fair.

Life wasn't fair, however, as her grandmother had often told her. No matter how hard you tried to do what was right and honest, things didn't always work out.

She had come close, so close to making a huge mistake there in the moonlit night. If things had turned out differently, she thought Lucca might have brought her back here to the palazzo and made endless love to her while the rain pattered down and Venice sank around them. Yes, and she would have let him.

She would, yes, she would indeed. Squeezing her eyes shut, she flung herself to her back, shivering with the chill inside her.

She had to be on her guard from now on. She couldn't come that close again. It would not do when it was extremely possible Massimo was her grandfather. If he was, that would make Lucca—what? Her first cousin? Or at least a half-first cousin if his father and hers were half-brothers?

No, it definitely would not be right. Certainly, it would not be, could not be while Lucca remained unaware of the possible relationship.

Should she tell him? Didn't he deserve that consideration? But what if he went to Massimo with the tale and she was sent packing before she could discover the truth?

Celina lay for hours, staring into the dark while her thoughts turned in circles. Dawn light was seeping around the heavy draperies at the French doors before she slept.

A dull roar woke her. It was long, sleep-drugged seconds before she recognized the sound. It was the generator Lucca had brought in for his restoration of the palazzo's façade. Steady, shatteringly loud, it was accompanied by a hard, regular thudding that seemed to jar the walls of the palazzo.

It was the end of rest. She was groggy and still tired beyond words, but it didn't matter. Throwing back the cover, she slid out of the bed.

The grand old palazzo seemed deserted when she descended the stairs. Massimo was not to be found, nor was Sergio or Lucca. Hot coffee and rolls were waiting in the dining room, but the others seemed to have eaten and gone about their day.

It was later than she'd first thought, she saw on checking the time; it was the gray pall of rain that made it seem earlier. She should set to work, should find what she had come for so she could settle her mind once and for all.

No sooner had she made that decision than she heard voices coming faintly from outside, raised above the clamor of wind, rain and machinery. Moving into the salon, she went to the French doors that led out onto the loggia. She pulled the curtain aside to look out.

Lucca, heedless of the blowing rain, was working with his crew once more. Wearing a heavy yellow slicker suit, shiny with wet in the brightness from a bank of working lights, he directed what appeared to be the driving of a series of pilings next to the landing. Massimo stood on the *fondamenta* with Sergio beside him, holding an umbrella above them both. He shouted back and forth with his grandson who was aboard the barge, balancing with the natural movements of a man who had lived most of his life on the water.

Lucca had no hood on his slicker suit, wore no hat. His hair was plastered to his head. Rivulets of water ran from the wet curls, trickling into his face and down the sides of his neck. His lashes appeared meshed together, and water dripped from the end of his nose. He looked commanding yet exasperated, and totally unlike the aristocratic gentleman of the night before. He was even more compelling in this setting, more viscerally appealing.

Hot longing poured through Celina, heating her face and breasts before pooling in the lower part of her body. She put her forehead to the facing beside the door and gave a low moan as she breathed deep against the pull of it.

This was not what she had come to Venice to find. It wasn't in the plan, didn't fit into wherever she might go from here. Maybe she should just leave now, before she did something she regretted.

But that was what her grandmother had done years

ago, run away before she could succumb to a desire as compelling as it was inconvenient.

Or had she?

Celina didn't know, and that was what was driving her crazy. She couldn't go until she discovered the truth, once and for all.

~ ~ ~

What was it with Celina? Lucca could not figure her out.

She blew hot and cold, melted into his arms and then withdrew until he was going out of his mind. He should probably walk away, but couldn't afford to do that as long as Massimo was involved.

He wasn't sure he could do it, anyway. It was as if he'd made a place for her inside his head, and now he couldn't get her out of it.

Something happened between the Campo de San Marco and the palazzo last night, something that changed Celina's mind. He'd been close to making her his, to turning her thoughts from his grandfather to him alone. Then suddenly the chance was gone.

She was attracted to him, he was sure of it. Her eyes were clear and approving when they met his. She responded to his touch, was warm and yielding in his arms. Yet there was a wariness about her that puzzled him as much as it intrigued him.

Most American women he'd known were not shy about asking for what they wanted, whether a meal in a fine restaurant or a night in bed. Not that there had been any great number. Girls from the States had been a fascinating novelty while he was at university, but he'd soon learned to steer clear. Brief and easy encounters didn't satisfy him, and he'd grown wary of the sexual daring that lay in the smiles of those sleeping their way through the European Union.

Celina was different. She might be drawn to him, but something was holding her back.

She wasn't about to tell him what it was; that much was obvious. His only alternative, then, was to stick close to her until he understood. Yes, or until whatever it was went away, and she came into his arms of her own accord.

It was strange, but as much as he longed for that moment, a part of him might regret it. He rather enjoyed her prickly attitude that kept him at a distance, their sparring back and forth with the zing of mental challenge. He liked her self-possession and lack of pretense, was pleased that she appreciated the palazzo without being awestruck by it. He genuinely liked her when he let down his guard.

That sneaking fondness was in addition to the drawing need of her that consumed him. His heartbeat turned uneven as he played the night before in his mind for the thousandth time. He'd been so lost in the perfect feel of her in his arms that he hadn't given a damn if high water drowned Venice and the two of them with it. The urge to have her in his bed, bare skin to bare skin, to touch and hold, to taste the sweet, tangy essence of her and feel her moist heat surrounding him, was so consuming he'd been astounded, unbelieving, when she vanished into the palazzo.

He wanted her still with a passion that destroyed his peace and threatened his sanity. And he meant to have her even if it ran counter to everything he believed or had been taught. Nothing was going to stop him.

Why had she run away? Why?

He had to find out.

He came upon her just before lunch. Notebook in hand, head down and scribbling, she was just emerging from one of bedrooms along the hall from his own. He'd had a hot shower to chase away the chill of working in the rain, and was still running his fingers through his hair to encourage it to dry as he left his room. He stopped, then turned to put his back to the door facing as he waited for her.

She paused as she looked up and saw him. She came on more slowly then, closing her notebook with the pen inside. Her face was set and eyes shadowed there in the dim corridor. Regardless, she was like a ray of sunshine with her pale, shining hair and a yellow cotton sweater worn with her jeans.

"How goes the appraising today?" Lucca asked, his voice carefully even as he fell into step beside her.

"Well enough, I suppose."

"Nothing of earth-shattering interest to report?"

"Not this morning." She gave him a quick glance. "I saw you working out front. Is there a problem of some kind?"

She had seen him. Had she looked for him, or was it an accident? He'd give much to know. He also realized her question was an attempt to deflect his interest in her job. That was a warning of sorts, but he would let it pass for now. "There was a storm with heavy rain in the Friuli region to the north. It's moving toward us and there's still a moon tide. That adds up to heavier flooding."

"Will it be bad? Is there anything I can do?"

"Are you serious?" He searched her face. An offer of help was the last thing he expected.

"I won't melt, you know."

He did know, too well. She had been deliciously firm in all the right places as he carried her to the powerboat last night. Climbing up and down ladders had not hurt her in the least.

To have her working beside him might be more than he could stand, nor was it necessary. He'd only pitched in on the pilings shoring up the landing this morning to work off his frustration after being so near her during the night, yet unable to reach out and touch her.

"No need," he said easily. "Everyone went to lunch, and I told them not to come back afterward. We've done all that's possible ahead of the high water."

A flash of something very like disappointment crossed her face then was gone. "But it was already rising last night, wasn't it?"

"It went down when the tide turned, but is a temporary retreat."

"So it will be back tonight?"

"Or sooner. It should be higher off and on over the next few days."

She nodded her understanding. The movement shook loose a silky strand of hair from where she'd tied it back.

The urge to reach out and tuck it back behind her ear so he could see her face better made his fingers itch. He was a tactile person; to refrain from that small act was almost painful. He thrust his hands into his pockets since he didn't want to press his luck. Still, he could feel his patience fading fast.

As they neared the head of the stairs, the enticing aromas of freshly baked bread and savory minestrone wafted to them from the dining room below. Lucca's stomach rumbled a little at the rich scent of the chill-chasing soup, but he ignored it. Coming to a halt, he turned to face Celina, blocking her path.

"What happened last night? Did I say or do something wrong?"

The glance she sent him was wary. "Nothing happened. The visit to the square was a beautiful ending to a night I'll never forget. I'm grateful to you for arranging it."

"You are suggesting..." He paused, uncertain how to phrase the possibility in his head.

"What?"

"That the kiss there in the square was just ... part of the service. A romantic end for a romantic evening."

Her indrawn breath lifted her breasts against the drape of her sweater. "I never thought such a thing."

"No? Then why run away afterward."

"Maybe I ran away because I felt I was being chased, but wasn't sure why."

She was right; still, he allowed himself a rueful smile. "You are a woman, I am a man. What else is there?"

"I'm not sure, though it really doesn't matter. The truth is I was tired and cold, and my feet were wet."

She stepped around him and started down the marble staircase as she spoke. Lucca moved to her side at once, ready in case she stumbled on the worn treads installed by some Victorian ancestor after he'd ripped out the original wooden steps. Marble as a construction material for staircases was not at all forgiving.

"That isn't an answer," he said, descending rapidly beside her. "I could have warmed you, even warmed your cold feet."

She stopped as she reached the bottom of the stairs. "Has it occurred to you I just wasn't ready for anything more?"

"It didn't seem that way there in the square."

"Maybe I thought things were moving too fast."

"Maybe you decided you could do better." He cursed silently as the words left his tongue. He hadn't intended to say such a thing.

"What's that supposed to mean?" she demanded while color receded from her face.

"Nothing. Forget about it."

"No, I want to know. You've had something on your mind all along. You may as well say it."

His gaze centered on her mouth as she closed her lips tightly together. The need to taste them again, to feel their silken heat and test the flavor of the lip gloss she wore, was like a sudden blow to the midsection. Her delicate scent of peaches and roses invaded his senses, taking his breath, wiping his mind clean of every thought except the need to be closer.

"You don't want to know what's on my mind just now," he answered finally, his voice a low growl.

She stared at him, her blue gaze probing, before swinging away in the direction of the dining room. "Fine. Don't tell me," she said over her shoulder. "I expect I can figure it out on my own."

She probably could, being both sensitive and intelligent, Lucca thought as he watched her walk away from him. And what he would do when she did, he had no idea.

Chapter Eight

"Celina, *cara mia?*"

She looked up from the notes she was taking while perched on the top step of her ladder. Her smile was immediate as she saw Massimo standing in the doorway of this back bedroom. His hands were thrust into his pants pockets, however, and his features were solemn.

"Is it dinnertime already? I've been so fascinated by this Tintoretto that I lost track."

"Ah, you've found the other one, I see." He came forward with slow footsteps to stand gazing up at her and the painting that loomed behind her.

"It was hardly lost, though you might have told me it was here."

"And destroy the pleasure of discovery for you? No, no, I would never do that."

A quick laugh sounded in her throat. "I'll admit it was a

pleasure to walk in on it, though there's been one thrill after the other since I began. You own so many treasures, Massimo."

"I am their custodian, let us say. This Tintoretto has never been a favorite, being a darker effort done after the death of his daughter. That's why it's tucked away in this back room." He frowned, rocking back on his heels as he considered her. "Aren't you cold in here where there's so little heat?"

"Too excited, though it is a little chilly now you mention it." She put down her pen and rubbed her hands together to aid circulation.

"So I should think. But no, it isn't yet time for dinner. Sergio has made coffee. I came to see if you would join me for it."

She was so close to being done in this room. If she finished, she could move on to the next in the morning. Besides, she didn't particularly want to see Lucca just now. "Is it a party?" she asked, as lightly as she was able.

"No, no, just the two of us. It will be a nice rest for you. That's unless you are anxious to finish so you can go home?"

"I'm close to being done," she said with an attempt at a smile. "And I don't want to wear out my welcome."

"There's no danger of that, *cara*, I promise. We will be sorry to see you go, Lucca and I. But we won't think of it while some few rooms remain to be explored."

She'd rather not think of it herself. "You are very kind."

"By no means, as I'm far too fond of having my own

way." He gestured toward the door, the skin crinkling around his fine old eyes as he smiled. "Now you must take a break. I insist."

Celina descended the ladder while Massimo held it steady. The uneasy feeling there was more to this invitation than appeared on the surface made her heart beat high in her throat. Her knees were none too steady as she moved ahead of him into the hallway.

They did not turn toward the stairs as she expected. Instead, he gestured in the opposite direction. At the end of that long corridor, he stopped at the door of the master suite which lay there. Pushing it open, he stood holding it for her.

She had not yet inspected this set of rooms out of consideration for her host's privacy. Her curiosity was keen as she walked inside.

The suite had a masculine air but with a Venetian difference, being done in soft blues enriched with rust tracery, and with heavy furniture that still had exuberant grace of form. The bedroom, seen through the sitting room doorway, was centered by a huge bed with damask bed hangings hung between soaring pillar-like bed posts that almost touched the ceiling. The window draperies were pulled back in both rooms, but framed only the dreary fading of the day.

Massimo snapped on a light, and then turned toward the fireplace with its gray marble mantel. A fire burned low on the hearth, lending welcome red-gold radiance as well as heat. Two wingback chairs sat before it with a tray table holding a coffee service between them. He went to stand in front of one, waiting for her to come forward and be seated in the other.

Celina didn't move. She was transfixed by the watercolor that hung above the mantel.

It was not large, but neither was it swallowed by its ornate gold frame. All the color and light and dancing life in the world lay within those borders, making it shine like a beacon in the bedroom's gloom. It was a view of Venice, one in which the Palazzo di Palladino held pride of place, with light gilding its walls, water reflections glittering on its windows and French doors, cat's paws of wind tossing the canal into leaping waves before it and pennants fluttering on the blue-striped poles at its landing. It was everything that was joyous and hopeful caught in delicately applied washes of paint. It was a Venetian summer frozen in time. It was a masterpiece.

It had her grandmother's style all over it, as well as her signature in the lower right corner.

"So," Massimo said with sad acceptance in his eyes. "This is, perhaps, what you have been seeking."

Celina moved as if sleepwalking, taking one mindless step after another. It was a moment before she could force words past the tightness in her throat. "It's the painting my grandmother gave you just before she left Venice, isn't it?"

"*Certo, cara.* Just as it was on the day I received it."

She'd known it had been painted for him all those years ago, had hoped to find it. Yet anything could have happened to it. It might have fallen victim to mold and mildew, faded away to nothing in too-bright light, or even been discarded as trash.

A tremulous smile curved her lips and tears rose to edge her eyelids. "She gave it to you, and in return you gave her a priceless Canaletto."

"Not a fair exchange at all as I valued her gift far more."

Such a graceful sentiment, but she did not doubt him, not really. "Your gift was the painting I found in her attic."

"Naturally," he said, his features shadowed. "I recognized the description of it at once, recognized your name on the article about it as well. It was simple to guess what must have happened."

"You knew me?" She moved to sit on the arm of the wingchair as she studied his face.

"But of course. I've had a deep interest these many years in anything that touched on Marilee, the lady who was your grandmother." A frown came and went between his brows. "You should have written to me directly instead of going through the auction house that employs you to make contact. You would have been made welcome at once."

"I didn't know that. You might have turned me away as some kind of con artist."

"Never." He reached to take her hand, holding it in both of his.

She could not help smiling at the certainty in his voice. "But if you had, I'd have lost all chance to see—"

"This one painting hidden away among all the others."

"I wanted to tell you, truly I did." She lifted a shoulder. "Even after I arrived, I couldn't be sure you remembered Marilee or had kept the watercolor she gave you—though I thought, once, that you were going to tell me about her."

"I almost did, but wasn't sure you knew of our connection."

"So would not destroy any illusions I might have about her?"

He made a quick gesture of dismissal for that bit of tact. "But yes, of course I kept her painting, also every newspaper and magazine article I could find that mentioned her."

"You mean—you're saying you followed her career?"

"And everything else I could glean of her life. Naturally, I only know what could be seen from the outside, nothing of what she thought or felt or dreamed."

Celina breathed slowly in and out as she absorbed the softness of his voice, recalled the inscription on the back of the Canaletto.

Forever.

"You wanted to know."

"You can never imagine how much." As if to distance himself a little from the hoarse pain in his voice, he released her and bent to the coffee tray, lifting the silver pot to fill the two cups that sat ready.

"I have her journals," Celina said slowly, "if you would care to read them."

He closed his eyes so tightly the lids trembled a little, opened them again. "Most gladly, if you will permit it."

She could not think of anyone who had more right. Inclining her head, she said, "I'll bring the one I packed, the most important one, down later. The others I can send to you. But I should tell you they have no great revelations.

Grandma Marilee was fairly discreet, maybe out of fear they would be read by the wrong person."

"I would expect nothing less of her."

Celina took a deep breath, let it out again. "In return, I would ask only one thing."

"And that is?" Massimo set the pot down with a gentle thud.

"I would like very much to have a closer look at this watercolor she painted."

"That's all?"

She met his gaze squarely. "I'd like to look at the back, if I may."

"Ah."

It was a sound of enlightenment, or something close to it. Thought sat upon his lined features as he lifted his gaze to the glorious scene of the Grand Canal on a summer's day, where gondolas plied the waters and a barge laden with a great pile of cabbages made its eternal way.

Celina waited, half afraid to say anything more for fear of tipping the balance of his decision the wrong way. It had come down to this, all the hopes and dreams that had brought her to Venice.

Even as she watched him, she was struck by the nobility of his profile, the strength in his features, the way he combed his hair back from his forehead that was receding only a little, allowing it to form deep, silver-white waves. This was the way Lucca would look in few decades, she realized. It was a fascinating insight, though she refused to consider why that might be.

Massimo released a sigh. Coffee forgotten, he stepped to the foot of the mantel. Raising his arms, he lifted the watercolor from its support and turned with it in his hands.

"Be careful," he said before pausing to clear his throat of an obstruction. "It's heavier than you might think because of the glass that prevents fading."

He was right. Celina was prepared, however, as she'd handled her grandmother's artwork many times before. Still, her fingers weren't quite steady as she accepted the weight and turned the frame to view the paper that sealed the back.

And there it was, just as her grandmother had written so many years ago. A few words and a date as described in the journal secreted in Marilee's attic for so many years, until it had come to Celina.

Forever, July 27, 1962, with a thousand regrets that I came to you only in my dreams.

Tears filled Celina's eyes, blurring the words. She'd known there was an inscription, suspected what it might say from Marilee's cryptic journal entry. But there had been no way to be sure until she saw it for herself. Now she was both glad and sorry at the same time for what it proved.

Yet the thought uppermost in her mind was the tragic waste of all the days Marilee and Massimo should have had together. Yes, and how different things might have been if her grandmother's long ago visit had come to a happier ending.

Massimo touched her shoulder in a gesture of comfort. "This is of such importance, to see what was written?"

"Oh, yes." She gave him a watery smile before looking down again, brushing her thumb over the words and date written in the rather elegant scrawl she would recognize anywhere. "You see it means—It means I'm not, cannot be, your granddaughter."

He stiffened a little beside her. "You thought you might be?"

"It seemed a possibility. My father was born early, just eight months after my grandmother's wedding day. What's written here makes it certain he was not your son."

"Someone suspected otherwise," he suggested, his voice a gentle rumble.

"The man she married, my grandfather, feared it for the rest of his life."

A pained expression crossed Massimo's face before he shook his head. "Did Marilee not tell him how it was between the two of us?"

"He accused her while she was still in the delivery room. She was so upset, so embarrassed and disappointed in him, I think, that she wouldn't give him the satisfaction of explaining."

Color mounted to his forehead, burned in the tops of his ears. "But surely this husband of hers knew she was untouched when they were married? I mean to say—"

"Apparently it wasn't that obvious," Celina answered, heat rising in her face as she caught both the contempt in his voice and what he was implying. "The wedding night was not—not a great success."

"He had no experience, this great idiot, this *cretino*, was clumsy and in too great a hurry."

"As you say."

Marilee had allowed some of her pain and frustration to seep into her journal. It had been possible to guess, reading between the lines, that she'd been a virgin, though it had never been spelled out in so many words.

Massimo whispered with the sound of a curse, and then fell silent.

Celina went on after a moment. "I suppose a part of it was that she'd told my grandfather, as soon as she returned to the States, that she could never love him, that there had been someone in Italy. I believe she thought he might call off the wedding. Instead, he said it didn't matter and insisted they be married anyway. But after the baby came early, he threw her Italian summer into her face every time they had an argument."

"How could she have done it?" Massimo asked with pained incomprehension strong in his voice. "The Marilee I knew was too intelligent to marry a man so wrong for her, one who would try to take away the light inside her."

Celina could not be surprised that he understood her grandmother's dedication to the magic play of light and need to bring it from inside her. It was what had driven her to buy the cottage as a place to paint, and to stay there so often and so long it became a form of separation from her husband.

"The wedding was already planned, the date set for just a week after her return," she said with a small shrug. "Everyone expected it, and the family pressure was hard to resist."

"Yes, I'm sure of it," Massimo said on a sigh. "Such pressure is not unknown here."

"My grandfather thought he could make her forget, or so I imagine. It didn't quite work out that way."

"So he became bitter. Such a fool, to take out on her what could not be changed."

"It wasn't only on her. He could never quite accept my father as his son, but still made sure he was formed in his image."

"Including despising his mother."

"His own mother, yes, and all—all other women." Celina swallowed on a sudden ache in her throat.

"Even you, perhaps? Oh, *cara*, I am so very sorry. I would have been proud, most proud, to claim you as my granddaughter."

A tear rimmed the edge of her lashes and spilled over making a wet track down her face. "I'm sorry, too. I would much rather have had you for a grandfather."

"Don't cry, *cara mia*." His voice was thick with emotion as he reached to wipe away her tears with the pad of his thumb. "Some things need not be of the blood. You are so like your grandmother who was more than life to me that I dare to think of you as the granddaughter of my heart."

She turned toward him in blind need. He gathered her close, despite the painting she held that lay between them like a piece of Marilee. Closing her eyes, Celina rested her head on his broad shoulder, absorbing the warm comfort and acceptance that was more certain than any she had ever known. Her heart swelled with the sensation, aching in her chest.

She had never realized how much she had longed for unquestioning approval until she felt it now. Her tears wet his shirt collar, and she breathed deep, letting it out in a pained sigh as she said goodbye to a dream. Somewhere inside, she had wanted Massimo Palladino to really be her grandfather. At least she had until she came to Venice.

"Is this a private party or may anyone join it?"

That question, stinging despite its quietness, jarred her like a blow. It was Lucca who spoke as he stood in the doorway Massimo had left open in an old-fashioned nod to propriety. His words were pleasant enough, but the cast of his face was grim and tension was clear in the set of his shoulders.

Massimo released her, but kept one arm at her back as he turned to face his grandson. "We were just having coffee while taking a look at this watercolor," he said evenly as he flipped it to face Lucca. "Do join us, give us your opinion."

"I've always thought it remarkable for its use of light and color, though it seemed modern for your tastes," Lucca answered with barely a glance at it. "But really, I can't stay. I only wanted to ask Celina if she'd like to go out to dinner later."

"Oh, I don't know," she began, glancing up at Massimo.

"Of course you must go. It will do you good to get out." He smiled down at her. "We will have time to talk more between now and then, if it pleases you."

"Yes, I would like that." Her smile was not quite steady

before she turned back to Lucca.

"If you prefer to stay here with Nonno—" he began before she could speak.

"No, no. I would also enjoy going out to dinner, only—only a little later."

He thrust his hands into his pockets as he pushed away from the door frame. "At eight?"

"Perfect."

"Until then."

Celina stared after him for an instant as he disappeared down the hall. He didn't understand, she thought; she would have to set him straight. She could do that now. At least, she could if he was at all reasonable.

Turning back to Massimo, she smiled. "Now where were we?"

~ ~ ~

It was necessary to wait while Celina showered and changed for dinner. Lucca wasn't surprised. She and his grandfather had talked for hours. He had heard the murmur of their voices and quiet laughter from his bedroom.

It had been a distinct jolt, coming upon the two of them in each other's arms. He could still feel the poisonous bite of it in his muscles. The situation might not have been quite what he'd first thought, but he'd no wish to see such a thing again.

He didn't think his heart could take it, seeing his nonno, for the briefest of seconds, as an aging satyr. Especially not with Celina in his sights.

Something would have to change, immediately, to make certain it didn't happen.

Celina was worth waiting for as she descended the marble stairs to where he waited at the foot. The dress she wore might not be a designer creation, but its lavender-blue fabric clung to her curves with utmost fidelity, the heart-shaped bodice was a perfect frame for her modest cleavage, and the flirty little skirt that swirled above her knees drew attention to spectacular legs.

Her hair swung in shining softness around her face, instead of pulled back as he was used to seeing it. Her lip gloss made her lips appear as luscious as peaches. He could not prevent the tightness in his chest as he watched her coming toward him, not to mention in other parts of his anatomy.

Lucca took the tan Balmacaan coat she carried and held it for her as she slipped into it. To caress her shoulders as he settled the coat into place, feeling their warmth through the all-weather fabric, was as natural to him as breathing.

In that moment, he had no thought whatever of his grandfather.

He took her to one of his favorite restaurants located no great distance away along the Grand Canal. A small and rather intimate place in winter, it had a wooden platform that floated in the water on pontoons, and served to double seating capacity during the summer tourist season. That section stretched damp and empty this evening, its tables and chairs stacked away in storage. It would be swamped at high tide, or even at low tide if a fast moving boat created a wash high enough. Diners were often warned to lift their feet if one approached.

"*Ciao, Lucca! Come stai?* Thank you for bringing this so lovely lady to my poor restaurant!"

It was the owner, Federico, round, bald and jovial, who called out the greeting. His smile held unqualified approval of Celina as he directed them to the table overlooking the canal, and she smiled as if she had more than an inkling of what he'd said. Presenting menus with a flourish, their genial host rattled off the specialties of the evening while shaking out Celina's napkin and draping it over her lap. He lingered then, exchanging pleasantries and complaints about the despised *acqua alta*. Lucca was beginning to think he would be with them all night, but the arrival of other customers took him away.

"You must come here often," Celina said as she watched Federico thread his way through the tables toward the entrance.

"At least once a week, though I'm usually waved to a table and left to fend for myself." Lucca's smile was wry. "The extra attention is in your honor."

"Very flattering, but I'm sure it's a restaurant owner's stock in trade."

"Not at all. You are a beautiful woman, Celina. Has no one ever told you?"

Wild rose color swept across her cheekbones with swiftness it pleased him to see, given his intentions. He wasn't quite as happy with the skepticism in the blue depths of her eyes. She made no answer, however, as their server put in a timely appearance with a basket of warm, napkin-wrapped breadsticks in one hand and a carafe of red wine in the other.

When the wine was approved and poured and they were alone again, Celina reached for her glass and took a small sip. She sent him a quick glance from under her lashes before she spoke. "I suppose you're wondering what that was about with the watercolor earlier."

Lucca had thought he might have to pry the information from her. That she brought it up herself put him on his guard. "I'm certainly curious."

"It was done by my grandmother, you know."

"I suspected as much." He played with his wine glass, turning it with two fingers while he watched doubt and pain and some odd, sweet sorrow play across her face. It was an effort to hold back instead of reaching out and taking her hand, offering comfort.

"She had it framed and wrapped, and then handed it to Massimo at the airport on the day she left Venice. She wrote on the back of it, a dated and signed message very like the one on the painting he'd presented to her a day or two before, when he knew she was going."

"A sentimental gesture, I suppose." The dry comment was the best he could do as he recalled the way Celina and his grandfather had held that painting between them as if it was the most precious thing on earth.

"Yes, well, people were more romantic then."

He could argue that point, but now was not the time. "So you saw this love note which proved—what? That your grandmother and Nonno were lovers?"

Her smile was so stiff it barely moved her lips. "The opposite, rather. It proved they never went that far, showed plainly my father could not be Massimo's son. By the same token, I am not his granddaughter."

Lucca felt as if a bomb had detonated under his breast bone. He was still for long seconds while thought shifted in his mind. When he spoke his voice rasped in his throat. "This watercolor is what you came here for, what you've been looking for all this time."

"It's fair to say that, though I was also more than a little interested in meeting Massimo."

"Having heard so much about him?" He'd suspected something similar at the ball, hadn't he? Her interest had always been too marked for a mere art appraiser.

"Not really. My grandmother never mentioned him while she was alive, though she talked now and then of her time in Italy. It was only after she passed away that I found the journal she kept during her Venetian summer. I think I told you about it before, her sketchbook with a multitude of canal scenes, palazzi, people and boats of all kinds? It also had notes on what she did day-by-day."

"And Massimo was there in it."

"Its most prominent subject. Judging from its pages, she loved him to distraction, though she never came right out and said so."

"She went away and left him instead."

"She was engaged to someone else, the wedding planned. Her family would never have understood if she'd suddenly announced she was in love with someone else. She couldn't abandon everything and everyone she knew to come and live in Italy. Or at least she didn't feel she could."

He drank a generous swallow of his wine and set the glass back down. "Nonno asked her to do that?"

"Apparently so. Whether he meant it is something else again."

Lucca gave a short laugh. "If he said it, he meant it."

She looked down, adjusted the position of her fork, and then looked up again. "I thought so, but couldn't be sure. Not that it matters after all this time."

"He told you he was committed as well? The arrangement between him and my grandmother was understood long before they married, so must have been in place during that summer."

She met his gaze, her eyes shadowed. "I didn't realize that."

"To have abandoned the commitment would have caused just as much of an uproar in Nonno's family." Lucca gave a small shake of his head as he thought of him risking so much for a summer flirtation with an American tourist. He must have loved her beyond all reason.

"I expect she knew that," Celina said, almost to herself, "especially if she met his family, as his sister said."

"You're thinking it would be another reason she decided to go?"

Celina gave a small nod. "Marilee would not have been comfortable taking her happiness at someone else's expense. It was the way she was brought up, the way she was."

"Another time, with different ideas."

She didn't answer at once, but turned to watch out the window as a police boat came tearing down the canal, two-note siren wailing. It swung wide for a left turn down an intersecting side canal across from where they sat, and then sped on. The wake it left behind washed up on the floating platform outside to lap against the wall beside them.

When the noise of the siren died away in the distance, she met his gaze again with quiet resignation in her eyes.

"Anyway, it didn't happen, just as nothing happened in Massimo's bedroom earlier. There's no need to be so annoyed about it."

Lucca lifted a brow. "Is that what you think I am, annoyed?"

"You're very protective of your grandfather."

"He was hurt once. I don't want to see it happen again. But there's more to it than that."

"Meaning?"

"He's seemed a little too affectionate."

"Don't be ridiculous!"

Lucca opened his mouth to explain, but the server arrived at his elbow to take their orders. The instant the man moved out of hearing again, Celina leaned toward him with blue fire in her eyes.

"Let me make this clear for you," she said, her low voice trembling with her disdain. "I came here for several reasons—to see Venice, to meet Massimo, for the honor of appraising his art collection, but also on the off chance I might lay hands on the painting my grandmother had given him. I'm not sure why you find this so hard to believe, but I assure you that's all there is to it."

"For you, maybe."

"What's that supposed to mean?"

"It's not been unknown for an older man to relive his youth, to try to go back to the way things were and make them turn out differently. You are a lot like your grandmother, or so it seems. What better way to make things right than with a May-December marriage?"

She leaned well back in her chair, putting distance between them. "You don't really believe that."

"Don't I?"

"You can't!"

"Maybe yes, maybe no." Even as he spoke, Lucca knew something in this situation still raised questions. He wasn't quite sure what it was or how Celina was involved, but he didn't intend to sit still for it.

No, it would be best if Nonno was edged out of the picture. That would be best, even if Celina wasn't interested in him other than as a grandfather figure.

He had to proceed with transferring her interest from Massimo to him, Lucca thought in hard decision. Toward that end, he needed to know more about her. Something inside him craved that knowledge, wanted to understand how she thought, exactly what she felt, enjoyed, dreamed or loved with all her heart. It was important in some way he could not quite grasp, yet trusted by instinct.

One thing that he'd learned this evening just might

make his goal easier.

"At least some good has come of all this," he said with dry appreciation.

Her expression turned wary. "And that is?"

He leaned toward her and touched his wine glass to hers with a musical chime while smiling into her eyes. "You've made it quite clear we don't share a grandfather, which means we aren't related. There is no kinship whatever between us, none at all."

CHAPTER NINE

It had turned cooler while they were in the restaurant. Mist rose from the water as they walked down the *fondamenta* that ran alongside the canal, a stealthy fog that crept from the water to roll against the building, getting thicker by the minute. Celina huddled into her coat, grateful for its all-weather protection against the damp chill.

Lucca seemed not to feel it as he strolled at her side, matching his pace to her shorter footsteps. His overcoat hung open, billowing a little with his movements, just as his ancestor's cloak must have billowed as he walked here long ago. Lucca was bare-headed, and the mist clung to his hair in fine droplets that turned the waves into unruly curls. Either he was used to the weather or else definitely a hot-blooded Latin. Celina thought it was probably the latter, as she sensed, now and then, a hint of his warmth wafting toward her.

A quick grin for that idea curved her lips. At that moment, they passed the lighted entrance of a palazzo that had been turned into a hotel.

Lucca glanced at her with a lifted brow. "What's funny? Something you'd like to share?"

"Not really," she answered, her humor fading.

"Like that, is it?"

His smile was rueful, as if he knew he was the source of her amusement. It was not unexpected. He had unbent enough to laugh at himself more than once during the evening, had been charm itself after their rocky start. No man she'd ever known had been as attentive, as quick to anticipate her needs or as interested in her slightest thought or opinion. She was half afraid she'd talked more than she should, certainly more than was wise.

"If you must know, I was thinking how much you must look like the seventeenth century Conte di Palladino, striding along here in the fog."

"You think so, do you? I'll have you know I'm at least a hundred millimeters taller and probably several kilograms heavier."

"You don't mean it."

"And there's no need to be superior, as I expect you are a bit larger than—"

"Careful," she said in mock warning.

"Larger than his lady. People are now, on average."

"True." It was easy enough to concede him that, given the camaraderie that had grown between them.

Her thoughts touched on his obvious satisfaction, back at the restaurant, for the idea that they were not related. What did that mean to him, exactly?

The question had plagued her off and on ever since. She knew the fact that her libido was not turning somersaults over a blood relative was a relief to her, but did he feel the same? Was he really attracted to her, or only being polite in a peculiarly Italian fashion by obligatory flirtation?

She considered asking him, but could not quite decide how to bring up the subject. Before she could work her way around to it, a disembodied voice came to them out of the mist.

"Gondola ride, Signor? Signorina?"

Two steps more and the gondola stand materialized ahead of them. Celina could just make out the black boats, jostling each other with the water movement. A gondolier leaned against the post of his stand with a heavy jacket over his black-and-white-striped shirt and a cigarette dangling from his mouth. He straightened, flipping the cigarette into the canal as they drew nearer. "A beautiful night for a romantic ride, Signor. I make you a good winter price, and a better one because of the high water."

"Oh, I don't think so," Celina said with doubt in her voice as Lucca's footsteps slowed. "Not at this time of night."

"The best time," he answered as he veered toward the gondolier. "Besides, it's a tradition. And I did promise."

So he had.

Celina was not thrilled, regardless. What could they see

in the darkness? She pushed her hands deeper into her coat pockets as she listened to Lucca bargain in rapid-fire Venetian and with emphatic gestures. She caught a little of it, as her Italian had improved dramatically in the past couple of weeks, but the city dialect was so different that most of it went over her head.

Agreement was soon reached and payment arranged. The gondolier whipped away the tarp that protected the seats from damp and held the unwieldy craft while Lucca handed Celina into it and stepped in after her. Leaping to his place on the rear platform, then, he shoved off. They glided away from the landing and out upon the waters of the canal.

It was a choppy ride caused by windblown waves, also by a series of troughs left by a passing water taxi. Lucca reached across Celina for a pair of lap robes that lay folded at the end of the low, burgundy velvet-upholstered seat. Shaking them out, he layered them together then spread them across their legs and tucked the edges in on either side.

Celina startled a little as she felt his fingers slide under her thigh. She thought they lingered an instant longer than necessary, but could not be sure. He was so close in that moment she caught the scent of damp linen, warm male and the spice and bergamot notes of his cologne. As he straightened, a small shiver moved over her at the sudden loss of his warmth.

"It's okay," he said, his voice a low murmur near her ear, "we'll soon be off the open water."

"Good," she answered, then clenched her teeth together to keep them from chattering.

Behind them, the gondolier bent to his job. Their progress was swift and quiet through the muffling fog, though the hum and roar of boat motors could be heard no great distance away.

Abruptly, they surged forward in a burst of speed. Celina swung her head to see a vaporetto bearing down on them out of the mist.

It swerved with a blast of its horn. Their gondolier sent a rude hand gesture after it as they swept forward into clear water. She shivered, and tried not to think of how easily the big, bus-like boat could have smashed the gondola to pieces.

A short time later, they left the main waterway and swerved into a narrow side canal. The water calmed at once. Motor noise faded away. As they penetrated deeper, everything was still, the darkness lighted only by an occasional landing lantern to guide some resident home.

It was amazing to Celina, the completeness of the silence. She should be used to it by now, as she had grown familiar with the winding pedestrian walkways closed to traffic. Somehow, she'd never noticed it in quite the same way. So total was it that she could hear the gurgle and splash as the gondolier plied his oar, the dripping of water from fog-wet balconies above them, and the sleepy cooing of pigeons disturbed by their passage.

"Where are we going?" she asked as she pulled the lap robes higher up under her arms.

Lucca's teeth flashed white in the semi-darkness as he

smiled down at her. "Nowhere in particular, just a circuit of back canals. It should take maybe an hour. Does it matter?"

"I don't suppose."

"Good." He watched her a moment. "Are you cold?"

The concern in his voice was enough to warm her, but she nodded anyway.

"Permit me."

He lifted his arm and placed it behind her back, giving a gentle tug that invited her to move closer. She shifted a little, easing into his welcome heat, against the firm muscles of his chest. There was security in his nearness. The night, the unstable boat, the murky darkness of the more remote canal they turned into, were not nearly as threatening.

Taking her hand, Lucca lifted it to his warm lips in a brief salute, and then tucked it under his coat against his chest. Her fingers clenched on his as pleasure suffused her. With it came a sudden floodtide of need. And that was more than a little strange when she wasn't entirely sure she trusted him.

He changed so quickly from anger to flirtation, from accusations to disarming care for her welfare. She was left feeling off-balance and wary beneath the hum of desire in her blood. Physical attraction knew no logic, however; it was simply there, irresistible, inescapable.

Yet there was peace in their swift, smooth progress, in watching the houses that loomed ghost-like above them as they snaked through the curving, mist-shrouded waterway. Disembodied voices came to them out of the gloom now and then, though it was usually long seconds before they reached the chatting strollers.

Lucca's body heat surrounded her, banishing her chill. Celina could feel his heartbeat, strong and vital, through the thickness of their clothing. His sheer masculine presence was disturbing yet compelling. Silent exultation rose inside her, seeping through her veins as she rested against him, so she felt more alive than ever before in her life.

Above them, the gondolier began to sing in a well-rounded tenor, a haunting rendition of *Torna a Sorrento*, 'Return to Sorrento.' The pure sound was amplified by the buildings that rose above them on either side, echoing like a solo in an over-large shower.

Celina felt herself smiling as she listened, and unconsciously leaned more into the man who held her. It was a perfect moment of the kind that should be frozen in time.

"What do you think now?" Lucca asked, tilting his head as he tried to look into her face. "Worth the loss of sleep?"

"Definitely. Thank you for the thought." She was touched by his concern. She was also, she knew well, being seduced by the sheer romance of the occasion and the night. Still, she refused to let it make a difference.

"It's my pleasure," he said, a deep note in his voice. He released her hand he held and touched her face with his fingertips, lifting her chin a little so his breath whispered across her lips. "My very great pleasure."

He kissed her while the gondolier segued into a lovely ballad she didn't know. She might have not have heard enough of it to recognize anyway, as her senses swam with giddy exhilaration.

The taste of him was honeyed madness; she could not get enough. He traced the moist surfaces of her mouth, delved deeper, abraded her tongue with tempting flicks of his that she followed in expanding wonder, returned in growing abandon. He was tender in his invasion, and yet relentless. She didn't want him to be any other way, didn't want him to stop. Not now, not ever.

Lucca skimmed a hand beneath the lap robe to draw her closer as they reclined on the low seat. His touch at her waist, spanning her rib cage, sent a tremor through her that destroyed thought, melted inhibitions. She caught the edge of his overcoat in her fist, tightening it so he was pulled closer. When that was not enough, she slid her fingers beneath the open coat's edge, seeking the muscular firmness and heat of his chest.

The gondolier held the last throbbing note of his song, drew breath, and then began an impassioned version of *Santa Lucia*. Lucca stirred with every sign of reluctance. Glancing upward to the man at the oar, he spoke in quiet command.

The song above them continued, but the gondola swung toward a landing just along the way. Bringing the long craft alongside, their gondolier leaped to the *fondamenta*, splashing up to his ankles in the water that covered it. Bending, he pushed the gondola off to send them on their way again.

"What is he doing? Where is he going?" Celina turned her head in time to see the gondolier tramping through the water in his rubber boots, heading back the way they had come.

"Allowing us privacy," Lucca answered with a trace of amusement and something more in his voice. "Don't worry. We'll drift along with the current."

"But how will we get back?"

"I'll use the oar or we'll walk. It's not a problem." He paused. "Is it?"

They were floating gently along. Their progress was not as fast as before, but was still a soothing, natural progression that banished both anxiety and care. She hesitated, then lifted a shoulder. "Not really."

"Excellent," he said with dry approval. "You grow more Italian every day."

She doubted that, even as she wondered how much he'd paid the gondolier to desert his craft and them with it. It would be no small sum, she was sure. That she could consider it was, she feared, the definite sign of a prosaic American mind.

Ahead of them appeared a line of steel racks topped by wooden boards. It stretched through the mist, disappearing down a footpath toward some campo beyond. She frowned at it a moment before turning toward Lucca.

"A walkway," he said before she could form her question. "This area of the city floods before that around the palazzo."

"You mean people use that walkway to get from place to place?"

"Exactly."

"The water under it looks as if it's rising fast. Maybe we

should go back."

"We will, soon. The high water is only here, in this area, for now."

The confidence in his voice banished her unease somewhat. She did her best to relax and accept the gentle rocking as they were pushed by the wind. She was far too aware of the man beside her, however, of his muscular thigh which lay alongside hers, also the taut expectancy that hovered between them.

It was sheer nerves that finally drove her to speak again. "You've done this before, I suppose."

His arms tightened a little where he held her. "Taken a woman on a private gondola ride, you mean?"

"And then dismissed the boatman. It must be the Venetian equivalent of parking a car and making out on the backseat."

"I hadn't thought of it that way," he said with a trace of amusement in his voice. "But no, it's not a habit of mine."

"Really?" She wanted to believe him. At the same time, she was disappointed by this move. It seemed calculated and entirely too sure of her cooperation.

"I swear it. Do you mind? Shall I call the gondolier back?"

Of course she minded. She was frustrated beyond words. Need ran through her veins like liquid fire. Yet the romance of the evening had faded. This was now about getting it on.

Or was it? What that possibility only in her mind?

"No," she said finally, "I suppose not."

He touched her face, trailing his fingertips along her jaw

to her chin, brushing the fullness of her bottom lip with his thumb so it throbbed with exquisite sensitivity. "Good. You don't have to be nervous. Nothing is going to happen you don't want."

His eyes were hollows of blackness, his features little more than a blur. She wished she could see him better, could know what was in his mind.

"And what about what you want?" she asked, the words a mere whisper of sound.

"It doesn't matter, as long as you are comfortable here with me."

Those quiet words were like a release. Her doubts seeped away as heated longing returned. "I am," she said. "And—and what I want is you."

She felt his muscles tense with surprise, or maybe shock. He whispered a soft imprecation that seemed half prayer before he spoke again. "*Certo*? You're sure?"

Was she? She'd known him such a short time, had no idea where they might go from here. She only knew she didn't want to make the same mistake her grandmother had made, didn't care to be so high-minded she missed this enthralling opportunity fate had arranged.

Fate? Or was it Lucca?

Oh, but did it really matter while the aching need to be held and loved flooded through her and her mouth tingled with the urge to feel his lips on hers again? When she wanted to *live* for once in her life, as her grandmother had always advised. Yes, even if she regretted it later.

As if on some cosmic cue, a siren blared out then in its

piercing, steadily increasing warning of rising water. The *acqua alta* was coming again. It seemed she could feel the lift of it beneath their gondola, sense it in the faster pace of its drift.

"Yes," she said in sudden, breathless certainty. "Yes—only hurry!"

But Lucca didn't.

He drew her to him with slow care, setting his mouth to hers with such exactness the two surfaces and their edges matched to perfection. His touch was everywhere, clasping, and cupping, learning her curves and hollows until her senses reeled with it. Enthralled by the concentrated attention and elusive sense that he was starved for the feel of her, she gave him access while trailing her fingers down his cheek, along his jawline and to the tucked corner of his mouth.

Beneath the covering of lap robes he made clothing fall away. She inhaled sharply at the first cool draft across her skin, yet aided him with trembling fingers, pushing his coat from his shoulders, pulling his shirt from his pants. The first, intensely gratifying brush of his hard body against her softness loosened her inhibitions so they floated away.

Mindless with need, she tangled her hands in his hair while he teased the nipples of her breasts with lips, tongue and careful teeth. She closed her hands on his shoulders, grasping until her fingertips stung, as desperate to hold him to her as he had been to touch her.

The heat and power of him was a sensual overload. She was on fire inside and out, her blood simmering in her veins. There was nothing and no one except the two of them there in the dark and dripping night. And that was before he pulled the lap robes up over his head, disappearing under their cover.

He held her to him, tasting, exploring with such concentrated expertise that she was soon mindless and gasping. She clutched his shoulders, trembled as she felt the smooth glide of his muscles under her palms. Her breasts swelled and every muscle tensed. Thought tumbled into delirium as she felt the wet glide of his tongue on her abdomen, and lower. Thorough, relentless in his commitment, he murmured his appreciation in liquid phrases, encouraged her soft moans.

Rising, rising like the moon tide, the moment came close, and closer still. Then her world came apart in a cataclysm like none she'd ever known. She turned her head from side to side with tears lining her lashes. At the shattering apex of it, she pulled him to her once more.

Hot skin to hot skin then, he sheathed himself and gathered her close. The joining was fluid, fiery and strong as he set the gondola rocking to a rhythm as old and natural as the sea.

This was no mechanical grappling fueled by rutting fervor. It was intelligent, controlled, and all the more intense for it, an endless engagement of minds as well as bodies. Her heart strained in her chest as she moved with him. Her breath rasped in her lungs. Pleasure spiraled up inside her again, a swirling storm of the senses. She convulsed against him, clasping him to her with every quivering muscle, burying her hot face in his shoulder as a silent cry of triumph and impending loss echoed in her mind.

And through it all, the siren screamed out the threat of high water.

~ ~ ~

Lucca sent the gondola gliding back down the pathway of canals. Standing on the aft platform, he used his whole body to wield the heavy oar against the current, pushing with hard, fast sweeps while silently cursing himself.

He was ten kinds of a fool. There was no other explanation.

He should have known better than to ignore the predictions for high water. He should never have taken Celina out in the gondola. Or having made that mistake, he should never have dismissed their gondolier.

Never, ever, should he have kissed her.

He could have turned back when she expressed her doubts. But no, he had to keep going. The first bleat of the siren should have been a signal to stop, but he hadn't heeded it. He should have refused her soft plea, kept his hands to himself, kept his clothes on, and never pressed his molten hot, naked body to hers.

He never should have set out to seduce her, for he was the one who had been seduced.

He should not have left his rubber boots at the palazzo, either. Given how fast the water was rising, they were going to have to wade home after returning the gondola. He'd considered bringing them in a carrying bag like most Venetians this time of year, but decided it wouldn't look macho or romantic.

Romantic. What a Figaro of nonsense.

Celina had relied on him to look after her, and this was how he repaid her. Not only had he made love to her where anyone might have looked out from an upper window to see them, but now he had exposed her to cold and wet. He'd be lucky if she ever spoke to him again.

Worst still, he'd failed to recognize her essential goodness, refused to accept her lack of guile. He'd suspected her of being either a gold-digger or a thief. He was still struggling with the odd connection between her and his grandfather, but could no longer believe she'd conned Nonno into doing anything he hadn't wanted.

He glanced down to where she sat on the seat below him with the lap robe pulled up to her chin. She'd combed her hair with her fingers, but it was still deliciously tumbled. The disorder could possibly be blamed on the wind if anyone was still up when they arrived back home, but Nonno was unlikely to be fooled.

Celina was too quiet. He'd give much to know what she was thinking, how she felt now. She wasn't the type to chatter away about nothing, but he preferred some acknowledgement that he was there behind her.

A fool, yes.

"Are you all right?" he asked, raising his voice above the gurgle and splash of the oar and the rush of the wind that funneled toward them down the channel between the houses. Misting rain had begun to fall. He could see it spangling Celina's hair when they passed an occasional lighted window.

"I'm good." She sent him a flashing smile, he thought, though it was too dark to be sure.

"It won't be long now. We're almost back to the Grand Canal."

"Yes, I see the lights."

So polite, but then he'd noticed she was always that. It was a charming and unexpected trait. Even when she made love, she—

But no, best he didn't think about that if they were to get home any time soon.

Of course, she could still be wondering at what had happened, asking herself what came over her that she'd invited it. She could be planning how she'd get rid of him when they reached the palazzo, as she had before. She was so unlike most women he'd known that anything was possible.

She was attracted to him, he was certain of that much. Well, she was attracted to the first conte, and he could hope he shared some portion of the same pull as his ancestor.

What would come of it, he could not say. Most likely, she would finish the job she'd come to do then go back to the States. At least he had tonight and whatever time was still left.

The waters of the Grand Canal were rougher now than before, an expanse of white-capped waves. He'd lived on the water all his life, had been running up and down the canals in boats of all kinds since before he was old enough to drive. The canal was hardly a problem, but he still had no time to think as he steered the pitching gondola across it.

To see their gondolier waiting at the stand to help bring them alongside was a distinct relief. That he was standing in water nearly over the top of his boots didn't help matters at all.

Lucca thought seriously about offering a hundred euro or so for those rubber boots. They would swallow Celina's feet, however, and probably make it harder for her to walk. With resignation and a sigh for his favorite loafers, he leaped to the dock with a great splash that wet him to his upper thighs then turned to help Celina make the jump to the landing.

She gasped at the water's chill as she splashed down into it, but didn't shriek or complain. He hugged her to him for an instant, pressing his lips to the top of her damp head in gratitude and silent apology. With a brief word or two for their gondolier, he turned with her. Taking her hand and placing it in the bend of his elbow, he started wading down the *fondamenta* with her, heading toward the palazzo.

The water swirled and eddied around his shins, which meant it was nearly to Celina's knees. More than that, she wore heels that made walking more difficult. She stumbled once, and he caught her before she went down.

"You're okay? You didn't turn your ankle?" He could hear the anxiety in his voice but couldn't help it. He kept his arm around her since it felt so right to have it there.

She looked up at him with laughter visible in her eyes

from the storefront just ahead of them. "I'm fine. Don't fuss."

"This isn't exactly what you're used to."

"But you are?"

He shrugged. "This is Venice."

"Which makes it all right, I suppose."

"I despise the *acqua alta*, but could never live anywhere else."

"It must be nice to be so grounded."

He hadn't thought of it that way, but she was right. He was Venetian, would always be Venetian.

They squelched along a few more yards, pushing their way through the water while it squished in and out of their shoes with every step. A wind gust swept the light, swirling rain toward them, also pushed a wave that wet them a good six inches higher than before.

"You're positive you couldn't live somewhere else?" She was looking up at him as she walked, her eyes sparkling as she teased him, her lips tilting in a smile.

Abruptly, she struck an uneven spot. Her heel turned, and she lurched, almost wrenching out of his hold.

Lucca cursed as he snatched her back. Bending, he put an arm under her knees and lifted her high against his chest.

"What are you doing? Put me down!"

"I don't think so."

"You can't do this."

"Can't I?" He pretended to consider that as he started walking again. "It would be easier fireman style."

She clutched at his coat, clinging with both hands. "Don't you dare!"

"Be still, *cara mia*, or we may both wind up in the canal."

She took him at his word, or so it seemed, for she was quiet during the short time it took to reach the palazzo. She had grown chilled, perhaps, for he felt her shiver, try to control it then shiver again.

Or at least he thought that was the reason. Dared not imagine otherwise.

At the lower door of the palazzo, he paused a moment. Bowing his head, he held Celina close, absorbing the feel and scent of her into some secret part of his body. Then he breathed out slowly and lowered her feet to the pavement while he took out his key and opened the door.

He half-expected Sergio, if not his grandfather, to be waiting up for them. Who could sleep through the blasting of the high water siren, after all? Yet no one was about as they stepped over the piled sandbags that protected the interior and swished their way through the water that had seeped into this ground floor area in spite of the barrier. A few yards over ancient stone rough with wet grit and they were able to make their way up the winding stair to the living quarters.

Even here, all was quiet. Taking off their shoes and leaving them behind, they made wet tracks across the end of the salon to the marble staircase. They mounted, dripping all the way—something Sergio would have much to say about in the morning. Outside the door to Celina's bedroom, they stopped.

"You should take a hot shower to get warm. You don't want to have pneumonia," he said, partly from concern but also to bridge the awkwardness that had risen between them since entering the palazzo.

"So should you." She glanced at him and then away again.

It was inevitable that his mind would put them in a shower together. He was a man, after all, and Italian on top of that. It didn't help that she seemed to have the same thought, from the way she colored and bit the inside of her bottom lip.

"Don't do that." He reached to rub across her lip with his thumb, tugging it free.

Her mouth curved at once in a brief smile. "I can't help it. It's a habit."

"Yes, when you are doubtful or puzzled or just concentrating."

"You noticed all that?"

He shifted a shoulder. "And much else."

"I'm flattered." She hesitated. "I think."

"I think of you more than you know," he said truthfully.

"I'm sure, wondering what my agenda might be."

Water was dripping from his pants legs to puddle on the floor around his sock feet. He ignored it in his focus upon her. "And what is that?"

"Nothing much, not now."

His attention sharpened. Did she mean since they'd made love or since she'd found her grandmother's watercolor. "Not now?"

"You know why I came here. For the rest, you'll have to ask Massimo. It's his story."

Leaning toward her, he braced his hand on the door frame. "I'd rather hear it from you."

She rested her back against the closed door behind her, but didn't try to evade him. "I'm sure you would."

Somehow, in the few seconds between his request and her answer, he lost the thread of what he was saying, also all interest in finding it again. The cause was the lush line of her lower lip that was still pink from where she'd mistreated it. That tender surface needed soothing, and he knew the perfect way to go about it. He studied the problem, glanced up to meet her eyes, and then looked at her mouth again.

There was no decision. Somehow his body inclined toward her the fraction required, and the next thing he knew, he had gathered her close and put his mouth to hers.

She was so sweet, so soft and moist, warm and pliant. He could not get enough of her unique flavor or the feel of her in his arms. He wanted to fill his hands with her, to press his skin to hers inch by chilled inch, to create friction between them until they were both steaming hot. He wanted to banish her shivering, to lie with her against him, over him, under him for all the night long, and maybe even longer. He wanted—

Dio, he just wanted her.

Lifting his head after long moments, he met her gaze that was darkly blue and not quite focused. "About that shower?" he asked, his voice so husky he almost didn't recognize it himself.

She didn't answer. Instead, she caught his hand, reached behind her for the door handle, and pulled him into her bedroom.

Chapter Ten

It was the click of the door closing that woke Celina. To open her eyes was an effort. It seemed she'd only let them fall shut seconds before.

The dusky light coming around the edges of the drapes at the French doors told her it was near dawn. She knew immediately what the sound must mean.

Lucca had left her bed and her room. He was gone.

It was for her sake, she was almost sure. He would not want to call attention to the fact he was sleeping with her. Massimo was of the old school, and would not approve of such behavior under his roof. He might regret it in his grandson, but could well blame her for allowing it.

She would far rather have awakened in Lucca's arms.

She swept a hand across the mattress, finding the lingering warmth where he'd lain. She opened her fingers wide to capture as much of it as she could, thinking of how the two of them had fallen asleep with legs entwined in the early morning hours.

But first, they had taken a hot shower to chase away the chill of that last, wet walk. They moved together under the stinging spray, sliding wet and warm against each other with fragrant lubrication from the lavender soap she'd bought at an alley stall.

He'd molded her breasts with gentle hands, brushing the tips to small, tight buds, and then measured the slender turn of her waist with his thumbs spread wide. Skimming lower, he captured the twin spheres of her backside and drew her close against him while smiling into her eyes through wet-spiked lashes.

She combed the black silk of his chest hair with her fingertips and smoothed her palms over the firm musculature underneath. Standing on tiptoe, she licked water from his lips, sipped it from his lightly bristled chin, loving the taste of flowers and Lucca. That was before she took his hard, soap-slick length between her two hands, also before he muttered a plea to the gods and hefted her up with her legs around his waist.

The sizzling, plunging friction of body against body in contrast with the icy marble tiles at her back was exciting beyond all reason. Never in her life had she felt more open or giving. Never had she been more attuned to another person or so very alive. The pounding glory of it shuddered through her, thundering in her veins. Straining, moaning deep in her throat while half-drowned from the water pouring over them both, she acknowledged her need of this, only this, from the banquet that was life.

Yet there was more, a kaleidoscope of sensations and images that made her feel hot all over just remembering them. That was after Lucca dried her with slow and beguiling devotion to every surface and crevice, and then carried her to the bed. It was a wonder he'd been able to drag himself from her room and back to his own so early.

Proof of male stamina, she supposed. She wasn't sure she could move.

A small smile twitched a corner of her mouth. She was spine-tinglingly aware of physical contentment. She wanted to bask in it for a little longer before she got up. Besides, she really felt almost feverish, and so tired her very bones ached with it.

She finally left her room some time later. Anticipation rose inside her as she went slowly down the stairs. With luck, she could still catch Lucca before he left for his office.

That was, of course, if he was going today. He might intend to work on the restoration. Or he could mean to spend this day with her, could have plans for showing her more of the city. She wouldn't mind seeing how high the acqua alta had reached during the night.

Voices reached her as she neared the foot of the staircase. They came from the dining room, a low rumble of controlled anger. It sounded like Lucca and Massimo in some kind of argument. She paused, reluctant to intrude, ready to retreat.

That was, until she heard her name.

If Massimo was taking Lucca to task for spending the

night in her room, he should know his grandson wasn't to blame. She needed to listen to tell whether she should make that clear.

She strained to follow the exchange in quietly virulent Italian, but was only able to catch the general outline of it. Massimo was saying something about the disrespect of seducing a guest under their roof, using an expression that seemed very like one she'd heard at home about birds fouling their own nest. She eased down the stairs a few more steps, until she could follow every word.

"It isn't like that!" Lucca said with anger in his voice.

"What is it like then? I find you creeping from Celina's room at daybreak, but am to think nothing of it? I'm to look the other way? No, and no again! One woman's life ruined by a Palladino is enough. You will not hurt Celina this way. I will not have it!"

It was strange to hear Massimo so near to shouting when he was usually so calm. Even more peculiar was the jangling thud that followed, as if he crashed his fist down on the breakfast table hard enough to make dishes and silverware rattle.

"One woman—"

"Celina's grandmother, Marilee, who gave to me the painting you saw before. Only she handed it to me at the airport and I never looked at it until she was gone. If I had seen what she had written even an hour before she left, things would have been different. But I did not, and so we both suffered. This will not happen to Celina."

"*Per l'amor di Dio, Nonno!* I have no intention of

hurting her!"

"What are you about then?" Massimo demanded. "Not so long ago, you could hardly bear the thought of Celina here at the palazzo. Now you are sleeping with her!"

"I changed my mind. Is that so hard to understand?"

"*Certo*, Lucca. From suspicion to seduction in the blink of an eye? It's too much. You do nothing without a reason. This I know well."

Silence fell in the dining room. Celina waited for Lucca's answer, her fingers where she grasped the stair rail numb from the tightness of her grip, the breath constricted in her chest as if cut off by a steel band. It was an eternity before he spoke.

"I will admit I thought at first to distract her, possibly remove her from temptation's way by turning her attention to me."

Celina clamped her free hand to her mouth to stifle her cry of protest. In that same instant, a chair scraped inside the dining room as if Massimo had leaped to his feet.

"*Porca!* You thought to remove her from my attention, you mean!"

"You must admit it was unusual, you bringing her here."

"I admit nothing of the kind! A girl a third my age? How could you think such a thing?"

"An art appraiser brought from the States at no small expense when Italy is full of such people? Come, Nonno, be reasonable."

"She is the granddaughter of the woman I loved long ago, *stupido*. It would be like incest."

"How was I to know? You were preening like a peacock."

"If so, it was nothing to you. How could you interfere in my affairs in such a way? You go too far, Lucca. You go much too far!"

Too far indeed.

Celina whirled and mounted the stairs again as quietly as possible. Her throat ached. She felt hot all over, yet was icy cold in the center of her being.

Lucca had deliberately set out to seduce her. All his caressing attention, his compliments and the time spent with her meant nothing. He might have said he was removing her as a temptation for Massimo, but she knew he'd thought she was after his grandfather in the beginning. What better way to prevent that than offering himself as a substitute?

Every kiss and tender caress had been carefully orchestrated for one thing only, and that was to get into her bed. He had made love to her as a distraction.

A distraction!

It had worked.

That was the sad thing, how well it had worked. He'd made her fall in love with him while he felt nothing for her in return.

She loved him.

How blind could she be? She'd been so content, so ecstatically sated from his kisses and the way he'd made love to her. She'd thought his tenderness and care meant something, had dared think he might be falling in love with her. She'd even indulged in a delicious, half-formed fantasy of staying in Italy, of never leaving the Palazzo di Palladino.

Foolish, ridiculous dreams. She should have known better.

Tears clouded her vision so she fumbled for the door handle of her room before pushing her way inside. She choked back a sob as she closed the door behind her and then leaned against it.

She had to leave at once. She didn't belong here anymore than her grandmother had all those years ago. Massimo was a dear, sweet man, but she had no place in his life. She had found out what she needed to know, and now it was time to return to the real world.

It was time to leave the dream. Time to leave Lucca. Time to leave Venice.

She was tired, so very tired. Pushing away from the door, she walked to her bed and dropped down onto the soft, comforting surface. With a low cry, she toppled over and rolled, burying her face in the pillow where Lucca had slept, breathing his scent as her hot tears soaked into its softness.

She must have slept, for it was night time when she woke. Her room was dim except for the pool of yellow light created by the lamp on the bedside table. She was no longer alone. Lucca sat on the bed next to her, holding her hand in one of his while he brushed her hair back from her forehead with the other.

"She has fever," he said to Massimo who hovered at the foot of the bed. "She was chilled last night, and I thought she was too warm when I looked in on her earlier. Now she's burning up."

Massimo frowned down at her with concern darkening his eyes. "Shall I call a doctor?"

"I think maybe—" Lucca began.

"No doctor," Celina said, forcing the words through the rasping pain in her throat, hearing the fretfulness in her voice but unable to do anything about it. "Not now. I have to go."

"Go where?" Lucca asked.

"Home. I've been here long enough." She tugged at her hand, trying to remove it from his grasp as she recalled all the reasons it was necessary to leave. But he would not let her go.

"You can't," he said. "You're ill. I should never have taken you out in the gondola last night."

"No, you shouldn't," she told him with complete seriousness.

"I am truly sorry."

"She may have the flu that's been reported," Massimo said, drawing her attention. "She could have picked it up at the masquerade ball."

"She should definitely see a doctor then," Lucca said with finality.

Celina moved her head from side to side. "I don't want to go."

"And you need not, *cara*," Massimo assured her. "Dr. Mariano is a good friend, and will come to you as a favor."

That wasn't what she had meant, but she couldn't find the words to explain. She looked at Lucca, watching the way the light glazed one side of his face with gold while leaving the other in shadow, the sheen of it in the waves of his hair, across the bridge of his nose, the surfaces of his mouth and prickles of his late-night beard. It reminded her of something, a painted image seen many times, though the reality of the man beside her seemed brighter, stronger, against the cotton wool that filled her mind.

Lucca looked up at Massimo. "Even her hand is hot."

"See if you can get her to drink something while I make the call," his grandfather said. A moment later, he was gone.

Her eyes were dry and burning. She closed them for an instant. The mattress dipped next to her, and a strong arm reached behind her back, lifting her against a firm, too familiar body. "Here," Lucca said. "Drink for me, please, *cara mia*."

She felt cold wetness against her lips and obediently opened her mouth. The water was ambrosia as it trickled down her parched throat. She shook her head when she'd had enough, and he took the glass away. Still, she kept her eyes closed. There was such comfort in being held. She didn't want him to let her go.

Perhaps he knew, for he rocked her gently, his chin resting on the top of her head. His low voice came to her, rough yet musical in soft Venetian phrases rather than classical Italian. She tried to translate them, but it was too much effort.

"You got up this morning after I left you, yes?" he asked after a moment. "You are dressed. Shall I take off your clothes? Would that be more comfortable?"

It would be wonderful. She wanted him to remove his clothes, too, and then lie down beside her while he drew her against him. But that would not do.

She shook her head, a single, quick negative, before she could find some reason to change her mind. "I can manage."

"Yes, I suppose so, though…" he paused with a whimsical smile, as if he'd thought better of some suggestion he was about to make.

She looked away from him. "I can do that, if you will step outside."

"Ah, but *cara*—"

"Now. Please."

He was quiet for long seconds. Then he got to his feet with deliberate movements. "*Certo*," he said, "if that is what you want." He walked from the room, closing the door behind him.

Celina watched him go while her eyes burned with unshed tears. What she had done was the right thing, she knew. Why, then, did it feel so wrong?

~ ~ ~

Something was wrong, Lucca knew, and it wasn't just fever from a head cold or influenza. There was more to it than that.

Celina looked at him just now as if she barely knew him. That was beyond disturbing when mere hours ago she had smiled sleepily into his eyes, circled his neck with her arms while her warm curves nestled against him from breast to knees, and offered her mouth for his kiss.

It didn't make sense.

Celina wasn't some flighty tourist looking for an intimate memory of her Italian trip. At least he didn't think so, though he had to admit the night before might have filled a page in most women's travel scrapbooks. The back of his neck burned as he thought about it.

Dio, making love in a gondola. What had come over him? Such things were not done. He'd never have attempted it if he hadn't been half insane with her sweet allure and his need for her.

She'd thought it might be his habit, had asked about it at the time. Maybe she thought him a lothario who thought nothing of getting naked on what amounted to a public street in Venice. Waking this morning, she was appalled by what happened, maybe distressed she had succumbed to what was undoubtedly a rare impulse for her as well.

She was disgusted with him, wanted nothing more to do him. She just wanted to go home.

He clasped the back of his neck with one hand while he bumped the wall behind him with the back of his head. His grandfather had called him stupid. Could be he was right.

No, he refused to believe the Celina he'd come to know could change so quickly. But what did that leave?

She blamed him for enticing her out into the damp night? She thought it was his fault they were caught in the rain so she was sicker now than she might have been?

Could be she was right. He certainly blamed himself.

It had been a mistake, the way he had gone about getting to know Celina. He'd crowded her, smiled, talked, flirted, kissed her, and touched her for all the wrong reasons. He'd thought of seducing her, had planned it in cold blood.

Dio, but nothing he had done in these past weeks came close to be being cold-blooded! The exact opposite, in fact.

Finding her with Nonno, watching them together, fearing what might be, he had gone a little crazy. It was the only explanation.

She could not go. He would not allow it, not with the way things were between them. He had a few days, perhaps, to persuade her to give him another chance. This time, he'd go about it for the right reasons, in the right way.

He would seduce her with kindness, yes, but also with the pure, burning power of his desire. She would have to be made of iron to resist.

He wanted her smiles and her kisses again. He had to have them. To fail was unthinkable.

He would not fail.

This would be a masterpiece of seduction.

Then they would see.

Chapter Eleven

The knock that sounded on Celina's bedroom door was quick and light. It would be the young maid who looked after the bedrooms. She'd checked earlier to be certain Celina was awake, made a fire in the room's fireplace, and promised to bring her breakfast as soon as it was ready. Celina had protested, but it went unheeded. Signor Lucca had ordered it, and that was that.

"*Avanti*," she called.

The door swung open. It was Lucca who stepped inside, though he held the door while the young maid entered bearing a laden tray. His dark gaze as he met hers was thorough in its appraisal. In his free hand was an enormous bouquet of roses in blended colors of pink and coral.

"*Buon giorno*," he said, his voice like velvet.

Celina felt her stomach muscles clench while her heart stuttered into a heavier beat. She pushed up to a sitting position in the bed. "What are you doing here?"

"I came to have breakfast with you," he answered with a smile of melting warmth. "Also to bring you these." He presented the flowers with a flourish. "I saw them as I passed the market this morning. They reminded me of you."

The rose stems were wrapped in green paper, but otherwise as natural as when cut from the plants. She could just imagine him carrying them while strolling along the *fondamenta* toward the palazzo. He would have done that without a thought for how he might appear, his essential machismo unfazed by the obvious sentimentality. She had to admire that in him.

It was also rather nice to be compared to pink and coral roses—or would be if she believed a word he said. She didn't. Not a word.

As much satisfaction as it might give her to throw them in the trash, however, it would be awkward in front of the maid. Taking the massive bouquet, she held it to her face, inhaling their intoxicating scent. She touched a fingertip to the dewdrops that still clung to their petals as an excuse not to look at him. "I'd have thought you would be gone by now."

His voice turned grave. "To the office, you mean? How could I do that without finding out how you are today?"

Whatever the doctor had prescribed had worked wonders. She was better, though her throat was still scratchy and a small headache lingered behind her eyes. Not that she would give Lucca the satisfaction of hearing her say so. "I'm fine, thank you."

"Good. You'll be able to eat something. You've had next to nothing since our dinner three nights ago. That isn't the way to get better."

If she didn't know better, she'd think he cared one way or the other. "I've been eating."

"Chicken broth and a bread stick or two," he said with a dismissive gesture. "Here is an omelet with prosciutto and toast with honey. You must have it while it's still warm."

Before she realized what he was doing, he reached to slide a hand behind her back, easing her forward as he pushed the bed pillows behind her. She stiffened at the sizzle of electricity down her spine, sensed his hesitation as if he felt it, too.

But then he stepped back and gestured for the maid to place the tray across her lap. He folded down its supporting legs, removed the vase filled with water that sat on one corner, shifted the plate and small silver coffee pot so they were balanced, and nodded his satisfaction.

The maid withdrew, though a small, knowing smile curled her lips before she closed the door behind her.

Lucca seemed not to notice. With concentration in his face, he took the linen napkin that lay on the tray, shook out its pressed folds, and draped it across Celina's midsection. Taking the roses she still held, then, he unwrapped their stems, removed the small tubes of water that had kept them fresh, and thrust them into the vase he'd set aside.

He seemed to have thought of everything. Did he have some special aptitude for the game he played or were all Italian as practiced in the game of romance?

Celina sat watching him in bemusement as he moved the roses to the bedside table where their fragrance drifted toward her on a current of air. A fraud he might be, but he was still incredibly agreeable to look at with his precise grooming added to a blue dress shirt with open collar and sleeves rolled to the elbows, and gray dress pants. The morning light through the window caught in the waves of his hair, teasing blue highlights from its darkness, while it outlined the bone structure of his face in clear, masculine perfection.

She sighed, closed her eyes and then opened them again.

"Eat, eat," he said with a glance over his shoulder.

Glad of something to distract her from her disgruntled thoughts, she inspected the tray, lifting the cover that shielded the omelet with thin slices of prosciutto on the side and another that protected a bowl of raspberries, touching the napkin that covered a small loaf of warm bread. Next to the pot of coffee was one of hot milk. It was enough for two people. There were also two cups.

"This seems to be your breakfast as well."

"Only if you feel well enough for company." He turned from fussing with the flowers, thrusting one fisted hand into his pants pocket. His face was set, watchful.

He was giving her a choice. Almost, it seemed he expected to be sent away. She should do exactly that. Yet how could she, when he'd gone to so much trouble? The edicts of politeness and fair play impressed upon her by her grandmother could be darned inconvenient at times.

What was he doing? Why was he here? He didn't really

want her, so it must be about sex. She was convenient, that was all.

A gracious invitation to share was beyond her. The best she could do was a clipped reply. "I told you, I'm fine."

"Are you really?"

Her smile was grim as she ran her fingers through her hair that was in desperate need of shampooing. "Do I look that bad?"

"You are beautiful, as always," he said simply. "But I think you have a headache."

"How did you—"

"It's in your eyes. One moment."

In her eyes. It was disturbing to know she had that much of his attention.

He turned to the bedside table, picking up the small bottles that sat there, scanning labels until he found the one he wanted. Twisting off the cap, he shook a capsule into his hand. He poured water from the crystal bedside carafe into its matching glass, and held both water and capsule out to her.

"I don't think I need that," Celina said doubtfully.

"Don't you?"

His voice was neutral, without coercion or demand, yet she could feel the force of his will urging her to accept what he offered. Her resistance wasn't just stubbornness, not really. She suspected she might need her wits about her, and wasn't sure how a painkiller might affect them.

She could hardly tell him that, however. And her headache seemed to be increasing with every second he stood waiting.

Taking the capsule, she swallowed it down with the water then handed the glass back to him. She lay back against her pillows, but was far from relaxed.

His smile of approval was like a benediction. Warmed by it, yet hating that reaction, she sat and watched as he set the glass aside then turned to the tray across her lap. Filling cups with hot coffee, he frothed it with hot milk poured from some distance above and then put one of the cups into her hands. He lifted off food covers, buttered bread, and positioned the fruit so she could reach it with ease. Then taking the other cup, he settled on the mattress next to her feet.

She sipped her *caffelatte*. It was perfect, of course. She inhaled the warm and fragrant steam that rose from it, feeling it soothe her sore throat. It was so quiet in the room that she felt a strong urge to just close her eyes and drift away.

"Thank you for the roses," she said to fill the silence.

"I'm glad you like them."

"They are gorgeous. But you must have been out early."

He drank from his cup while lifting a shoulder. "I couldn't sleep."

He'd no doubt left the house for a paper and an espresso in some coffee bar, maybe even the one they'd been to after she was followed that day. "Why not? A guilty conscience?"

"Possibly."

She met his gaze with blank surprise. An admission was the last thing she'd expected.

"I know I should have brought you straight home the

other night instead of keeping you out in rain, taking you for a gondola ride and then letting you become chilled."

A corner of her mouth turned down as she remembered what else he'd done. Still, fair was fair. "You didn't talk me into the gondola ride. I went of my own free will."

A brief flare of some fierce emotion—gladness? Satisfaction?—lit the darkness of his eyes before he shielded it with his thick lashes. "Nevertheless, I apologize most sincerely. I should have known better."

Were they talking about the same thing? She couldn't tell, but it seemed best to pretend he meant exactly what he said.

"I don't suppose it's your fault I'm not used to Venetian germs."

"You don't blame me for this?" He gestured toward her sick bed with his coffee cup.

"Did you think I might?"

"You didn't want me around a few days ago."

He appeared unperturbed, but she could see the firm ridge of muscle in his jaw where he clamped his teeth together. An odd sensation settled in the pit of her stomach, one very like remorse.

"Yes, well, I wasn't exactly at my best," she answered finally, then waited with some distress to see if he would pursue it.

"And now?"

"And now I feel like a fraud, sitting here having breakfast in bed when I could as easily have gone downstairs."

"Doctor Marciano was concerned. He thinks you should

stay in bed another day."

"It's nice of him to be cautious, but whatever he gave me was apparently powerful stuff. I'll get up in a bit."

"Perhaps."

He meant to discourage it, but she refused to let that bother her. She needed to get up and get back to normal. She had to be better so she could leave.

He glanced at her untouched plate with a furrow between his brows. Then he gave a short exclamation. Leaping up, he set his cup aside and went quickly into the bathroom. She heard water running. Seconds later, he reappeared with a washcloth in his hand.

Celina opened her mouth to ask what he was doing, but it was clear enough as he seated himself beside her again and reached for her wrist. Lightning skittered up her arm at his firm grasp. Removing the coffee cup she held, he set it on the tray. A moment later, he began to wash her hands with the warm, wet cloth.

"You don't have to do this," she said, her voice higher than it should have been.

"I want to do it," he said, his gaze steady as he smiled into her eyes.

He was very thorough about it, sliding the cloth scented with lavender bath soap along each finger and in between them, over the backs, across the sensitive palms. Her fingers grew warm where they had been chilled before, taking on the electric heat of his hands as well as the warmth from the cloth. That sensation crept up her arms and into her chest, threatening to melt the coolness around her heart.

It also rose into her face, mounting to her hairline. She tugged against his hold, disturbed by the rising intimacy between them, needing to escape in purest self-defense.

His grasp tightened on her wrist and his movements stilled while his gaze fastened on her face. It seemed for a moment he would not let her go. She felt her heartbeat increase and tensed as she wondered if he could feel its wild throb in her pulse.

His gaze flickered over her, coming to rest on her lips. She realized abruptly that she was biting the inside of the bottom one again, and released the grip of her teeth.

A brief smile came and went across his mouth. He lifted her hand to his lips for the briefest salute, then let her go and turned away. Tossing the cloth toward the bedside table, he returned her coffee cup to her.

"Is there anyone you'd like me to call about your illness," he asked, his gaze shuttered and voice a bit gruff, "anyone who might be concerned at not hearing from you?"

She wished he wouldn't be so caressing or seem so concerned. His seduction of her was complete. He didn't have to keep on with it.

"No, not really," she answered. "I sent my mom a text last night."

"Your mother?"

He lifted a brow as he reached to break off the end of the bread loaf then took a piece of prosciutto to tuck into it. "From your closeness to your grandmother, and the way you inherited her property, I assumed you lived with her."

Celina, drawn by the scent of the paper thin ham, put down her cup and made a small sandwich of her own. The bread was still warm, its crust crisp while the interior was soft, the perfect accompaniment for the flavor-dense prosciutto. It was a moment before she could speak again.

"My parents divorced when I was seven. My mother took a job in a high-end clothing store and became a buyer. I spent a lot of time with Grandma Marilee."

"Your mother left you with her mother-in-law? Wasn't that unusual?"

She made a dismissive gesture with her small sandwich, even as she picked up her coffee cup again. "I never thought much about it. My mom's family was from Canada, too far away to be helpful. She and Grandma Marilee had a lot in common, I suppose."

"It must have been hard for you."

"Not really. I loved being at the cottage. Grandma Marilee was forever starting some new craft project or cooking something unusual. We traveled, too, just the two of us, to so many places."

"Not the usual grandmother."

She smiled while the warmth of memories curled inside her. "You could say that."

"You were an only child?"

"I was. Apparently my mother didn't care to bring another into a marriage that was going nowhere."

He ate another bite of his breakfast, swallowed. "She knew that early on then."

"Soon after I was born. I didn't look at all like my dad,

you see."

"Children often don't," he said with the lift of a brow.

"That was not my father's understanding. But then, neither had it been my grandfather's."

"He accused your mother of being unfaithful."

She looked away while old pain shifted inside her. Why she was telling him these things, she wasn't quite sure except he was a good listener and she needed something to ease the strain that hovered between them. What did it matter, anyway? Another day or two and she'd never see him again.

"He had no great appreciation for women," she said finally. "He certainly never trusted them, and that was on top of having a temper. My mother—I think she decided to have an affair because she'd been accused of it so many times she felt she'd already paid the price. It also gave her an out, a reason for my father to divorce her. He'd threatened to kill her if she left him, but it seemed it would be all right if he left her."

"A risky solution, I'd say."

"It was, yes. But he only put her in the hospital."

Lucca said something under his breath in extremely idiomatic Venetian. When he looked up at her again, sympathy warmed the dark depths in his eyes. "It's no wonder you have problems trusting men."

Her chin came up. "I don't have problems."

"No? You knew all the time that my grandfather and your grandmother had a relationship, yet you didn't breathe a word of it to me until you had what you wanted."

"It had nothing to do with you." She didn't have problems with trust. It was men who promised the moon then backed away when there was a problem.

"Didn't it?" he asked, a sardonic note in his voice. "We won't debate that, but you didn't mention it to Nonno, either, not at first."

"He knew who I was."

"But didn't realize you were aware of the connection. What did you think he would do if you leveled with him? Call off the appraisal, put you out of the house?"

She hunched her shoulders as she dropped what was left of her bread and meat onto her bed tray in sudden loss of appetite. "I couldn't chance it, not after coming so far. Besides, it all came out soon enough."

"Soon enough for you," he said, the words more than a little grim.

"At least I found out what I needed to know." She leaned her head back and closed her eyes. She recognized the move for what it was, a way of avoiding argument, avoiding dealing with Lucca. She didn't want to talk, didn't want to think. Not just now.

It might have been a minute or two later, but could have been more, that she heard him move; felt him hovering over the bed. Her coffee cup was taken from her lax grasp. Then he picked up her hand, and she felt the brush of the washcloth, cool now, as he wiped bread crumbs and the scent of ham from her fingers.

It was too much. Snapping her eyes open, she snatched the cloth from his grasp. She used it with a couple of quick movements and tossed it onto the tray.

"Done then?" Those words in his deep voice were controlled, neutral.

She tipped her head in assent, and the tray was lifted away. She didn't look to see what he did with it. Closing her eyes again, she concentrated on keeping her breathing steady and even. With any luck, he would think the pain medication was taking effect and leave her alone.

Instead, he came closer. She felt the wafting of an air current as he leaned toward her.

"You can't shut me out or keep putting me off, *cara*," he said quietly. "I won't allow it."

Hard on the words, the smooth warmth of his mouth touched hers.

If she'd had time to think, to remember or doubt, she might have turned away. As it was, she opened to him as naturally as breathing, needing that contact as she'd needed nothing else in longer than she could remember.

It felt right, so very right with its hints of tender caring and sure claiming. She felt the glide of his tongue against her bottom lip where she so often caught it between her teeth. She reached for him, catching the collar of his shirt to hold him to her. And the contact went deeper, was sweeter, richer than any she'd ever known. It pushed thought from her mind, leaving behind only a frightening yearning.

He touched her face, trailed his fingertips down her neck, caressing the pulse that throbbed in the hollow of her throat. It was that gentle testing, and the greater force of the kiss that resulted from it, that brought her to her senses.

She stiffened, released him with an abrupt, openhanded gesture. In the same moment, she turned her head away.

"I ... You shouldn't," she said, latching onto the first thought to flit across the turmoil of her mind. "You'll catch my cold."

"Not likely." He straightened without haste. "Unlike you, I'm used to Venetian cold germs. But even if I did catch it, it was worth it."

Tears stung the back of her nose with an acid ache. Why did he have to be so perfect? She swallowed with difficulty as she shook her head. "I'd rather not be the cause."

"Too late." His smile was rueful, though the look in his eyes was dark with some alternate meaning. "It was too late even before the night in the gondola."

She didn't want to think about that, refused to do it. Looking away from him, she drew a deep breath. "Yes," she agreed as she let it out in a silent sigh, "I suppose it was."

~ ~ ~

Celina's kiss had tasted of goodbye. Lucca didn't like that about it, though the hot sweetness beneath it made him desperate to climb into bed with her and never get up again. He longed to feel her molded against him, to fill his hands with her curves and revel in the flavor and scent of her until he could find her in the dark of night by those alone. If she thought the threat of catching her head cold was enough to stop him, she had a lot to learn about Venetian determination.

Besides, whatever Dr. Marciano had given her had

worked wonders. Her skin was cool to the touch and the feverish glaze had left her eyes. She could probably get up if she really wanted, but he didn't intend to aid and abet it. The longer she stayed in bed, the better it would be. At least the less likely it was she'd leave. He could stand the thought of her there, soft and warm and so very accessible, better than he could stand watching her go.

He still didn't know what he'd done that was so wrong. It worried him, but he was better with it than he'd been before. She couldn't kiss him like that, with such instant and open response, if he'd done anything too damaging. Could she?

Something had changed between them; that much was clear. He would not rest until he found out what it might be. If it took unfair means to discover it, then so be it.

"You just came from seeing Celina?" Massimo asked as he looked up from his game of solitaire laid out across an inlaid table in the salon. "How is she this morning?"

"Better." The answer came out shorter than Lucca intended in his preoccupation. Hearing its echo in his head, he added. "At least it seems so, though she didn't eat much of her breakfast."

"She'll eat when she's hungry. The main thing is that she gets enough fluids, at least according to Dr. Marciano."

"He called this morning?" Lucca waited, his heart suddenly accelerating, for the answer.

"I called him, rather," Nonno said with a shrug. "He expects a quick recovery. Celina is young and healthy and, so he said, in good hands."

"His, he means, as her doctor?" Skepticism edged the question.

"Possibly." His grandfather could not quite hide his smile.

Lucca picked up the red queen of hearts from the deck his grandfather had set aside and placed it on the king. "Tell me something," he said abruptly. "When you discovered the note Celina's grandmother left you on the reverse of the painting, why didn't you go after her?"

Massimo sighed and transferred his gaze to the fire that burned on the hearth. "I've asked myself that a thousand times, especially during these past few days. The answer is that things were not so simple then. Marilee was American and far from home. It was possible she would change her mind, forget what was between us, once she returned to her family. Then we both had obligations, promises made before we met. Such things are no longer of major consequence, but they were wrapped up with words like honor, duty and obligation then. In the end, I suppose it was just that—well, times were different."

Lucca gave a slow nod. "What she wrote on the painting was important, but she didn't say she loved you."

"No, not in so many words."

"So you had no idea how much she might care, and if it was enough."

His nonno sighed again. "Exactly."

It was what Lucca feared, that not knowing. He refused to accept the same eternal uncertainty.

Chapter Twelve

Night came after an endless day, dropping in a gray veil of misting rain and fog over Venice once more. Celina set the tray that had held her dinner out in the hallway and then locked her bedroom door. It was not that she didn't trust Lucca to stay away, not really. It was rather that she didn't want to lie awake waiting to see if he would come.

She'd discovered the limit of her resistance to him. She preferred not to put it to that kind of test.

His concern and attention to her comfort that morning had nearly undone all her good intentions. His smiles had been so tender, his touch made her long for things she was better off without, while the scent of the roses he brought her were a constant reminder of both those things.

He was devastating in his charm when he wanted to be. The trouble was, she had no idea why he bothered, now, after he'd gotten what he wanted.

Thinking about it made her weepy and weary. It also left her tired beyond words. It was the depression of disappointment as well as being ill, she was fairly sure, but all she wanted to do was sleep. The sound of rain spattering on the balcony outside added to the compulsion.

She lay listening to it, staring into the firelight-tinged dimness while reliving the kiss Lucca had given her that morning, tasting again its sweetness and unabashed passion. That could not be counterfeited, surely, and yet it meant nothing. He could want her without love, couldn't he?

That would be enough for many women.

She needed something more, ached for it deep inside in a place she'd hardly known existed until a short while ago. She wanted forever, the kind of eternal love her grandmother had found in Venice. If she couldn't have that, it was better to have nothing at all.

A faint sound pulled her upward through thick layers of sleep, away from a disturbing dream in which she and Lucca were both lost in night fog, passing each other unseeing, never quite touching. It came again, a quiet rattle from the canal beyond the French doors to the balcony.

She sat up, every sense painfully alert. She could hear the rain that still whispered and clattered as it fell relentlessly onto the balcony and canal below it, but that was all.

Throwing back the covers, she slid out of bed, adjusting her plaid flannel sleep pants and T-shirt that had twisted around her. The fire under its marble mantel had burned down to coals, leaving the room in semi-darkness. The faint glow of a neighbor's security lamp outlined the French doors. She moved to them on bare feet. Lifting the draperies aside, she stared out.

A man was climbing over the balcony railing. For a brief moment, her mind flashed to the flirtatious gondolier Lucca had warned her about nearly two weeks ago. Then something in the width of the man's shoulders, the grace of his movements, brought a sharp exclamation to her throat.

Her heart leaped against her ribs and her skin felt fiery hot. That purely physical recognition was annoying beyond words. She swept the draperies aside, grasped the French door's curled handle and pulled it open.

"What do you think you're doing?" she demanded.

Lucca, balancing astride the wide marble railing, had the audacity to grin at her. "Climbing up, as you can see. I thought of serenading you, but the whole point was to not wake Nonno. That same reason made standing below and acting out a Romeo scene a bad idea. That and maybe falling out of the gondola."

"You came in a gondola?" She had to look, she couldn't help it. Stepping onto the narrow balcony, she peered down to where one of the long black boats bobbed in the water, attached to a railing baluster by a four-pronged climbing hook clipped to the end of a rope. The rattle of that hook as it was thrown up and fastened must have been what awakened her.

"Don't come out," he exclaimed. "It's raining."

"What about you?"

"I'm already wet, not that it matters."

He was certainly that. Even in the dimness, she could see dark splotches on the shoulders of the sweater he wore and raindrops spangling the waves of his hair. She put a hand on her hip. "I don't know what you think you're doing, but you need to go away."

"Your door was locked."

"I know that. I locked it."

"You didn't answer my knock."

"Did it occur to you I might have been asleep?"

He lifted a shoulder. "Maybe, but I couldn't be sure."

"Or that I might not want company?"

"I had to see if you were okay."

That was considerate of him, or would be if she believed it. "If you think you're coming inside, you can think again."

"I'll only be a second, just long enough to be absolutely sure you're all right."

"I'm told you, I'm fine. Goodnight." She swung around and stepped back into the room.

"Celina, wait!"

Springing from the railing, he caught the door before she could close it. As she spun to face him, backing away, he stepped inside. He pushed the glassed panel to behind him, shutting out the rain.

"You were right, you really are wet," she said, moistening her lips as she noted the way his jeans clung to his thighs, a plain enough sight even in the room's shadowy dimness. "You should get changed."

"Good idea," he said, and reached to catch the bottom of

his sweater, tugging it up before stripping it off over his head.

"I didn't mean here!"

He dropped the sweater, reached for the top button of his shirt. "Why not? I'm suddenly freezing."

She couldn't see his face clearly, but there was a tremor in his voice. Whether it was from being chilled or private laughter was impossible to tell. "Your room is just down the hall."

"But Nonno might see me leave. I'd rather not risk that as he wasn't too happy before."

The excuse was glib, but carried a coaxing sound that sent a primal shiver down her spine. No matter, she wasn't about to stand there and watch him get naked. With heat rising in her face, she backed away, then whirled and skimmed into the bathroom.

For the briefest of seconds, she caught sight of her face in the mirror. Doubt and anger lay in her eyes, but beneath it was the hectic brightness of exhilaration. With a jerky movement, she flung away from the sight. Reaching for a towel on the nearby rack, she stripped it off and stamped back into the bedroom. Rolling it up in her hands, she sent it flying at Lucca's head.

His thanks was muffled as he buried his face in the soft terry cloth and then rubbed it vigorously over his hair. He slung it around his neck, then reached for the first button on his jeans.

"Stop!"

"Why?" His fingers made short work of his fly. "I don't

have anything you haven't seen already."

That was undoubtedly true after the night they'd spent together. "I don't care. I want you out of here."

"You wouldn't send me back out in the rain."

"Yes, I would." She put every ounce of conviction she could muster into that answer.

"You could never be that cruel," he said, stepping out of jeans and boxer shorts. Leaving them in a wet pile, he skimmed the towel over his lower body. "It just isn't in you."

"You don't know me."

"I think I do, maybe better than you know yourself."

She opened her mouth to answer. Before she could speak, he tossed the towel at the bathroom door and stepped to her bed. She caught a flash of firm, muscled backside before he slid between the sheets.

"Lucca!"

"Don't just stand there," he said as he whipped the covers back in invitation. "You'll be as cold as I am, and it might take drastic measures to warm both of us again."

She shouldn't go anywhere near him, she knew that very well. There was no future in it. All he was offering was the shared warmth of two bodies, a few moments or hours of pleasure. And yet, he wanted her for now, and yes, she wanted him.

"I thought you were checking to see if I was okay," she said, her voice tight.

"Yes, but it will be better by touch. With my hands, mouth and every inch of this cold body I long to touch you, Celina. I need to touch you, to hold you now, before I die of it."

How was she to resist such a declaration? It meant little beyond his desire of the moment, she was almost sure, but was everything to her.

Or it would have been everything just three short days ago. Now she knew why he wanted her, and it had nothing to do with his need to touch her, whatever that might mean. She didn't belong in Venice, had no place in the life of his grandfather. He needed to be rid of her in the fastest, least troublesome way possible. She had made that easy by falling in love with him. Yes, she had. But that was the end of it.

It was the end of it, and why not? He had promised her nothing. Nor had she asked for anything more than the moment. He was free and so was she. She could have this time with him if she was willing to accept it under his terms. Her every fiber longed for the ecstasy of it, for the warmth of his arms, his tender yet urgent kisses. She felt a little unsteady on her feet with the strength of that yearning.

She couldn't do it. No, not even as a fervent goodbye. She preferred her memories of the brief, shining hours when she'd thought he meant it.

"Celina?"

Puzzlement lay beneath the appeal in his voice and in the darkness of his eyes. He lowered his hand, shifted higher on his elbow.

She couldn't meet his gaze a moment longer. Turning away, she spoke over her shoulder. "I don't think I can let you do that."

"What are you saying? What is it?" The sheets and comforter slithered against each other with a sighing sound as he sat up.

The only way she could resist the sensual pull of his presence, naked in her bed, was to make him angry. That should be easy enough. All she had to do was let him see her own quiet fury that lay behind the pain swelling inside her chest.

"It would be different if it wasn't just a cheap sham. As it is..." Her throat closed off, preventing speech.

"A sham."

"Don't think I don't appreciate the effort you went to, because I do. I enjoyed every moment of it, St. Mark's Square in moonlight, the *carnevale* ball, the good food, the handsome company, and especially the gondola ride. I'll ... I'll always remember my time here."

"You're going." The words were tight and hard, as if forced through clenched teeth.

"Of course I'm going. I was never meant to stay."

"But I thought—"

"What?" she asked when he stopped. "That I would remain to finish cataloging Massimo's art collection? There are hundreds of art experts in Venice who can do the job. You told me so yourself."

"He will be hurt if you leave so soon. He's more than fond of you, you know."

"And I'm fond of him. That's one reason it will be best if I leave now. It will hurt less if we don't become too attached to each other."

"So that's it. You're running away." The mattress creaked on its frame as he left the bed. An instant later, she heard the rustle of his damp jeans as he stepped into them again.

"There's a difference between running away and just going home," she said evenly.

"Is there?"

"What I came here for is done. We're done."

"What happened, Celina? Did I get too close? Did you feel too much so are running scared?"

"I don't know what you're talking about."

"I think you do. You're uncomfortable with men. You don't trust them, won't let them into your private thoughts, don't want them too near you."

"Don't be ridiculous. Just because I—" She stopped, pressed her lips together. She wasn't afraid of men, she wasn't.

"You what? Had your holiday romance, something to talk about once you're back in the States? A little Italian fling in romantic Venice, complete with all the trappings? It was fine for a one-night stand, but now you're ready to call it quits?"

Shock rippled through her, fueled by the bitterness in his voice. "It wasn't like that!"

"How was it then? What am I supposed to think?"

He had moved in close behind her, so close she could feel the heat of his body. At least being furious with her had banished his chill. Fear that he would touch her, try to take her in his arms, made her whip around to face him with her hands knotted into fists.

"I know what you did," she said with outrage and pain strong in her voice. "You thought I was after Massimo, so you decided to—let me see, what was the phrase?—to distract me! Yes, that was it. You meant to show him how easily I could be swayed from one wealthy man to another who happened to be younger and good-looking. You did exactly as you said that first day when you told me you would prevent it—*no matter what it takes.*"

"Celina—"

"Well, fine. You succeeded," she said, her voice rising as she hit her stride. "But don't try shifting the blame or looking for convenient excuses for why I'm not panting to fall into bed with you. I'm just not interested in being *distracted* again, thank you very much. I've had enough. Got it?"

He was perfectly still there in the gloom while long seconds ticked past. Then he put out a hand as if to touch her. "Celina, I promise—"

"Don't!" She stepped swiftly away, crossing her arms over her chest. "Promises are the last thing I need. Just leave. Get out of my room now."

He swore under his breath then leaned to scoop up his shoes. "I'll go, but this isn't over."

He was wrong. Celina knew that perfectly well, as she watched him move from the room with strong grace, sliding through the open French door and out onto the balcony. She heard his shoes thud into the gondola outside, the rattle of the rope as he went down it. Then came the quiet splash as the boat pulled away, disappearing into the night.

It was over all right.

It was all over.

~ ~ ~

How could she go without saying goodbye to Massimo? Clearly, that was impossible. She owed him for so many things, for his belief in her expertise, his kind and generous hospitality, his understanding of her quest and his aid with it. It would be ungrateful to leave without a word.

She was ready to go. Packing had been no problem as she had not slept at all. By daybreak, she had compiled the figures and notes for the appraisals she'd finished and saved them to a memory stick for Massimo. She'd also used her laptop to arrange a direct flight to the States. Methodically folding clothes into her suitcase, filling plastic zipper bags, padding breakables with laundry, she tried not to think.

She had not added much to her wardrobe while in Venice. The only problem was the *carnevale* costume with its full skirt of iridescent illusion, its mask and elaborate wig.

She lifted the dress, held it close against her while dancing a few steps, whirling around with Lucca in her mind. Then she drew a deep breath and shook her head. Putting the whole ensemble away in the back corner of the *armadio*, she shut the door upon it.

Sergio, when she came down the stairs, said she would find Massimo at breakfast. She stilled herself to face Lucca, but Massimo was alone.

"*Cara, buon giorno,*" he said, rising to his feet. "Come sit down. Eat something. Five minutes earlier, and you could have had breakfast with Lucca. He will be devastated to have missed you."

Her relief was so great her shoulders sagged with it for an instant. Pulling her rolling suitcase into the room behind her, she twirled it around and left it beside the door.

Massimo smiled benignly as he gave her the ritual kiss on either cheek, but then he glanced toward where she'd left her luggage. A frown creased his forehead.

"But what is this? Surely you aren't going?"

"I think I must," she answered with a wan smile. "I've done what I came to do, and now it's time to go home."

"But this I cannot allow. You've only just arrived!"

"I'm sorry, truly I am. I wish I could stay, but there are things—it's really best that I leave."

He gave her a stern look. "You and Lucca have quarreled. He has done or said something foolish, and now you are determined to go."

He knew exactly what his grandson had done; there was no need to burden him with complaints about it, or with her hopes and disappointments.

"No, no," she said as lightly as possible. "There's really nothing between us."

"For sure? But I so hoped there would be."

She'd suspected as much from the way he sent them off together. "It's dear of you to say so, but—well." She stopped, cleared her throat. "You will tell him goodbye for me, please, and give him my sincere thanks for—for being my guide to Venice?"

"*Certo, certo*, but it will be much better if you do this yourself."

"There's really no time," she said, trying for another smile. "I have an early flight."

"But you must see him. He cares greatly for you. Do not ever doubt it."

The kindness in that attempt at reassurance was nearly her undoing. "No, really. It will be better this way."

Massimo's shrug was a masterpiece of Italian regret, sorrow and acceptance. "You must have a coffee and something to eat before you go."

"You're very kind, but I'll find something at the airport if there's time."

"Airport food," he grimaced. "But very well. Come, I will walk out with you."

Sergio was hovering in the doorway when they moved in that direction. Celina thought a quick look passed between the two men before the manservant took her rolling suitcase and moved ahead with it.

Outside on the *fondamenta* there was a delay. Massimo insisted she wait while he sent Sergio back for an umbrella, as he said he could feel rain in the air again. Afterward, he tried to persuade her to let Giovanni get out the powerboat to run her to the canal stop for the Piazzale Roma, where she must take a taxi to the airport. She argued against it, finally compromising by allowing Sergio to summon a water taxi for this first portion of her journey. When it appeared, idling its way up to the landing, she turned to Massimo one last time.

"You must come again, *cara*," he said, his voice gruff. "Do not forget. And do not forget us."

She agreed. What else could she do? Still, her smile was wobbly and her hug was tight as she kissed him on either cheek, for she was sure she would never see him again.

Then she and her suitcase were in the water taxi, and it was pulling away into the canal's main channel. Celina looked back as long as she was able, watching Massimo grow smaller and smaller with distance through the blurring of her tears.

The taxi plowed its way along, wallowing in the waves of larger boats, skimming around the curves. Celina swayed with the movement, hardly noticing, having grown so used to it during her stay. Nor did she notice the red tile-roofed buildings, the water traffic or the pedestrians in their rubber boots and Armani suits. She saw nothing, thought nothing. It was better that way.

It was raining, just as Massimo had predicted, when she stepped from the taxi at the last canal stop. A fine, blowing drizzle, it dimpled the puddles on the *fondamenta*, whispered in the canal as she walked alongside it, and pattered against the umbrella Massimo had provided. The wet weather suited her mood, though she shivered a little with its chill.

A bridge rose up ahead of her, one that crossed over a side canal before leading to the departure area for transport to the mainland. It was slick with rain water that stood in the indentations in the stone steps left by thousands of feet through eons of time. She struggled a little in the soft leather clogs she wore, slipping now and then as she dragged her suitcase up the risers of the high hump that allowed water traffic to pass under the bridge. The crossing wasn't really that steep, but neither was it easy in the rain.

But then she was over and headed down, her suitcase thumping behind her. A minute or two more of walking, and she could see the Piazzale Roma up ahead. She crossed a busy intersection with other commuters, spotted the rank of waiting taxis a short distance away. Soon she would be at the airport.

Venice lay behind her, a magical world eternally floating on its myriad reflections in the waters provided by the Adriatic. Back there was Massimo and Sergio, the Grand Canal and the palazzo. Back there was Lucca.

She was leaving them all. She was leaving, just as Marilee had done so many years before. She was going back to where she came from, returning to a life that seemed colorless and dull after the glory of Venice, to an endless round of days that were all the same, would always be the same.

She was going back to a place where no one kissed her hand, bought her gelato as a treat, or gave her armloads of roses they'd chosen and carried home because they looked like her. Back where no man would wear a costume of aqua silk because it was the color of her eyes, or make passionate love to her in a gondola floating down a public canal because she was irresistible.

He cares greatly for you. Do not ever doubt it.

What if Massimo was right?

What if there was some other reason she didn't know behind Lucca's actions, something that might make a difference? He'd wanted to explain, and she had been so certain she'd been duped that she refused to listen.

What if she was allowing her father's suspicion and lack of trust or affection to color her attitude toward Lucca, making her afraid of being hurt, afraid to chance her heart for the sake of a loving future?

What if doubt, pride and anger were forcing her to the same choice Marilee had made out of doubt, fairness and duty?

What if, like her darling grandmother, she was running away from her one chance at happiness?

What if this was a flight she would regret for the rest of her life?

So Lucca had seduced her for his own reasons. Didn't all men seduce their way into the hearts of women? Wasn't sexual need as much a part of what brought them together as undying fervor of the heart? Wasn't it the tap root from which love grew?

Not that she expected such an outcome, and yet women were the ultimate optimists, always willing to hope.

She had fallen in love with Lucca. Would it make a difference if he knew? Could she risk telling him, risk the hurt that would follow if it didn't matter at all?

Could she live with herself if she didn't take that chance?

Swinging around, dodging pedestrians, keeping her suitcase close behind her, Celina ran back toward the bridge.

It was even more slippery now than it had been earlier, and it seemed her suitcase had grown heavier. She had to manhandle it up the stone steps while juggling her shoulder bag and umbrella. It caught near the top, and she turned with a sharp exclamation, using both hands to dislodge it while balancing the umbrella handle between her chin and her shoulder.

Abruptly, a man reached to catch the suitcase handle. A quick tug and it easily came to rest on the step where she stood. She whipped the umbrella away, uncertain whether the helper close beside her side was a Good Samaritan or would-be thief.

Neither, it seemed, for it was Lucca.

He was hatless and had rivulets of rainwater streaming from his wet hair. The shoulders of his overcoat were soaked, and his fine leather shoes were water-logged.

"What—?" she began.

"What am I doing here? Nonno had Sergio call me, of course. Did you think he would not?"

"I didn't think at all. I just—"

"Apparently not!" He lifted both arms and let them fall. "*Dio*, Celina, what possessed you to go like this when you've been ill? How could you leave in the middle of what was between us?"

"I don't know what you mean."

"How could you leave me when I love you? I love you, Celina," he shouted, shaking his hands before him as if supplicating the fates. "How can you go when I love you?"

It was an excellent question, especially as she met the

hot espresso blackness of his eyes with their sparks of purest gold and felt the shift of something elemental inside her. A laugh rose in her chest, floating out clear and free on the damp air. His declaration was outrageously Italian, and she adored it. She adored that he was shouting his love in public without caring a bit that anyone and everyone could hear.

"It isn't funny, *cara*! I will not let you leave. I will not play Massimo to your Marilee, standing aside like an honorable idiot while you fly away from me. And I won't let you make yourself sick again in this twice-damned rain. "

"No," she said, still smiling as she angled her umbrella to cover both of them. "But you are wetter than I am. "You're the one who will be sick."

"I am never—" he began, then sneezed, started to speak, and sneezed again.

"Anyway, I couldn't go," she continued, a rising note of humor in her voice as she watched him pull a handkerchief from his pocket and scrub it down his face before wiping his nose. "I was coming back."

He glanced beyond her, looked down at her suitcase and the steps of the bridge where they stood with its foot traffic dividing and passing around them. "You were?"

"I decided I wanted to hear, after all, what you have to say about this grand seduction of yours."

He thrust the handkerchief back into his coat pocket while a frown drew his brows together again. "Then you should have stayed to hear what else I said to Nonno the morning you heard my confession."

"There was more?"

"*Certo*, much more, including how my plan backfired so I could barely think for wanting you. Also, *per Dio*, how you seduced *me* on that first day, when I saw you standing on that rickety ladder admiring the conte."

"I did nothing of the kind!"

"But you did, *cara mia*. I was so bewitched I couldn't think straight. I convinced myself I had to divert your attention from Nonno. He thought I was only playing at love, when what I wanted was for you to look at me the way you did him, as if I might be the answer to your prayers. I wanted you, even when I thought you might be after his title and position. My need was even more desperate when I guessed you hoped to find a place in the family as his granddaughter. And though I knew how much it meant to you, I was glad from the bottom of my heart when you said you were not of our Palladino bloodline."

"You didn't want me in the family?"

"Oh, I wanted you in the family, all right, but not as my cousin too close for comfort, and especially not as the future Contessa di Palladino. Well, at least not for the current conte and not for a long time. I wanted you as my wife, the woman whose portrait will one day hang in the Palazzo di Palladino along with all the rest, and who will be honored as my beloved until Venice sinks into the sea."

"Your wife." She had not expected it, not really. She wasn't sure what she'd hoped for instead, unless it was simply to be with him a little longer.

"Why else do you think I risked so much?" he demanded

with fire in his eyes. "I am no gondolier, constantly making love on the water or climbing to convenient bedrooms. You make me do crazy things, Celina!"

A smile curved her lips once more, one she could not stop. "I do?"

"You do." He met her gaze, his own warm yet daring. "But I think, perhaps, I do the same to you."

"Yes, you do," she said on a low laugh of delight. Reaching out, she caught the soft silk of his tie and pulled him close to set her cool lips to his. A groan sounded in his chest. Then he closed her in his arms, deepening the kiss until it warmed them both.

And the winter rains came down, spattering on the umbrella that covered them, falling softly into the canals of Venice.

END

Did you miss any of the other
ITALIAN BILLIONAIRES romances?

THE TUSCAN'S REVENGE WEDDING
(Book 1 in The Italian Billionaires Collection)

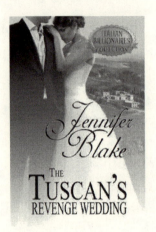

Revenge can indeed be sweet...

When her brother's car plunges off a cliff with him and his fiancée in it, Amanda Davies gets the news personally from the fiancée's brother. The devastatingly handsome Italian businessman appears in Atlanta and whisks Amanda off to Italy to be with the hospitalized couple. But could his motive be more?

Nicholas de Frenza never approved of his sister's choice in husband to begin with, and now that Carita is in a coma due to her fiancé's reckless driving, it seems the perfect time to resurrect an ancient Italian custom of revenge: the seduction calls for a similar seduction in return, a sister for a sister. But Nico is too civilized for such vengeance—or is he?

Even as Amanda falls for the Tuscan's charms, she knows his code and his family would never approve of her as more than a simple dalliance. But then the secret about the car wreck comes out—and that's when everything changes...

THE AMALFITANO'S BOLD ABDUCTION
(Book 3 in The Italian Billionaires Collection)

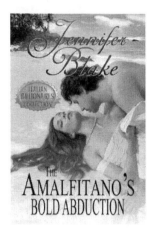

Dana Marsden's first mistake is stopping on the fog-shrouded Amalfi Coast road to help clear a traffic jam. Her second is rescuing the valuable cat that appears out of the mist. And the third? Trusting the handsome Italian who comes to her aid when her rental car plunges over a cliff in what may not have been an accident.

Since the American police officer refuses to believe she's in danger, Andrea Tonello sees only one option: spirit her away to the safety of his private island.

But who's going to protect him from one mad, independent lady when Dana discovers what he's done?

About the Author

National and international bestselling author Jennifer Blake is a charter member of Romance Writers of America and recipient of the RWA Lifetime Achievement Award. She hold numerous other honors, including the "Maggie", the Holt Medallion, Reviewer's Choice, Pioneer and Career Achievement Awards from *RT Book Reviews Magazine*, and the Frank Waters Award for literary excellence. She has written 73 books with translations in 22 languages and more than 35 million copies in print worldwide.

After three decades in traditional publishing, Jennifer established Steel Magnolia Press LLC with Phoenix Sullivan in 2011. This independent publishing company now publishes her work.

FMI: http://www.jenniferblake.com.

You can also find Jennifer on Facebook, Twitter, and Pinterest.

Find Jennifer's books on Amazon at
http://www.amazon.com/Jennifer-Blake/e/B000APHHS8

More Titles by Jennifer Blake

Louisiana Knights Series
Lancelot of the Pines
Galahad in Jeans
Tristan on a Harley
Christmas Knight *(A Holiday Novella)*

Contemporary Romance
The Tuscan's Revenge Wedding
The Venetian's Daring Seduction
The Amalfitano's Bold Abduction
Holding the Tigress
Shameless
Wildest Dreams
Joy and Anger
Love and Smoke

Sweet Contemporary Romance
April of Enchantment
Captive Kisses
Love at Sea
Snowbound Heart
Bayou Bride
The Abducted Heart

Historical Romance
Silver-Tongued Devil
Arrow to the Heart
Spanish Serenade
Perfume of Paradise
Southern Rapture
Louisiana Dawn
Prisoner of Desire
Royal Passion
Fierce Eden
Midnight Waltz
Surrender In Moonlight
Royal Seduction
Embrace and Conquer
Golden Fancy
The Storm and the Splendor
Tender Betrayal
Notorious Angel
Love's Wild Desire
Sweet Piracy

Romantic Suspense
Night of the Candles
Bride of a Stranger
Dark Masquerade
Court of the Thorn Tree
The Bewitching Grace
Stranger at Plantation Inn
Secret of Mirror House

eBOOKS:

Box Sets
Contemporary Collection Volume 1
Contemporary Collection Volume 2
Classic Gothics Collection Volume 1
Classic Gothics Collection Volume 2
Italian Billionaire's TwinPack
Louisiana History Collection Volume 1
Louisiana History Collection Volume 2
Love and Adventure Collection Volume 1
Love and Adventure Collection Volume 2
Louisiana Plantation Collection
No Ordinary Lovers
Royal Princes of Ruthenia
Sweetly Contemporary Collection Volume 1
Sweetly Contemporary Collection Volume 2

Nonfiction
Around the World in 100 Days (with Corey Faucheux)

Novellas
Queen for a Night
A Vision of Sugarplums
Pieces of Dreams
Out of the Dark
The Rent-A-Groom
The Warlock's Daughter
Besieged Heart
Dream Lover

Contact Jennifer Here:
Jenniferblake001@bellsouth.net

Or follow her here:
http://jenniferblake.com
https://www.facebook.com/jennifer.blake.3914
https://twitter.com/JenniferBlake01
http://www.pinterest.com/jblakeauthor
http://www.amazon.com/Jennifer-Blake/e/B000APHHS8